HERGÉ
★
THE ADVENTURES OF
TINTIN
★
TINTIN IN AMERICA

EGMONT

The TINTIN books are published in the following languages:

Alsacien	CASTERMAN
Basque	ELKAR
Bengali	ANANDA
Bernese	EMMENTALER DRUCK
Breton	AN HERE
Catalan	CASTERMAN
Chinese	CASTERMAN/CHINA CHILDREN PUBLISHING
Corsican	CASTERMAN
Danish	CARLSEN
Dutch	CASTERMAN
English	EGMONT UK LTD/LITTLE, BROWN & CO.
Esperanto	ESPERANTIX/CASTERMAN
Finnish	OTAVA
French	CASTERMAN
Gallo	RUE DES SCRIBES
Gaumais	CASTERMAN
German	CARLSEN
Greek	CASTERMAN
Hebrew	MIZRAHI
Indonesian	INDIRA
Italian	CASTERMAN
Japanese	FUKUINKAN
Korean	CASTERMAN/SOL
Latin	ELI/CASTERMAN
Luxembourgeois	IMPRIMERIE SAINT-PAUL
Norwegian	EGMONT
Picard	CASTERMAN
Polish	CASTERMAN/MOTOPOL
Portuguese	CASTERMAN
Provençal	CASTERMAN
Romanche	LIGIA ROMONTSCHA
Russian	CASTERMAN
Serbo-Croatian	DECJE NOVINE
Spanish	CASTERMAN
Swedish	CARLSEN
Thai	CASTERMAN
Tibetan	CASTERMAN
Turkish	YAPI KREDI YAYINLARI

TRANSLATED BY LESLIE LONSDALE-COOPER AND MICHAEL TURNER

EGMONT
We bring stories to life

Tintin in America
Artwork copyright © 1945, 1973 by Editions Casterman, Paris and Tournai.
Text copyright ©1978 Egmont UK Limited.

Cigars of the Pharaoh
Artwork copyright © 1955, 1983 by Editions Casterman, Paris and Tournai.
Text copyright © 1971 Egmont UK Limited.

The Blue Lotus
Artwork copyright © 1946, 1974 by Editions Casterman, Paris and Tournai.
Text copyright © 1983 Egmont UK Limited.

First published in this edition 2007 by Egmont UK Limited
239 Kensington High Street, London W8 6SA
This edition published in 2011

ISBN 978 1 4052 2895 4

Printed in China
5 7 9 10 8 6

TINTIN
IN
AMERICA

Chicago, 1931, when gangster bosses ruled the city . . .

Right you guys, listen, and listen good . . . Tintin, world reporter number one is coming here to clean up. That's tough on us, and I'm not kidding! He busted my diamond racket in the Congo and landed my pals in the cooler . . . So here's the score: not one single day does he spend in Chicago . . . OK?

Here we are, Snowy! . . . Chicago!

We'll go straight to the hotel.

Watch out, Chicago, here we come!

The Osborne Hotel, please . . .

There you go!

SLAM

Shutters down! . . . Sucker's walked right into the trap!

?

Hey, what's the game? . . . we're locked in! . . . And these shutters are made of steel!

We're stymied then. Even I can't chew through those!

BANG

A blow-out! That's all I need!

Come on, come on! . . . I gotta hurry up . . .

All fixed . . . I'll still make it in time . . .

Have a good trip! Lucky I packed the right kit . . . He'll go through the roof when he finds I cut my way out!

Trust me to be in the land of the automobile and have to slog ten miles on foot! . . .

We're in luck! Here comes a police patrol . . .

Quick, can you catch that car you just passed, and arrest the driver? He tried to kidnap me!

Just keep still, Snowy, and don't be frightened . . .

This way we'll soon overtake that gangster!

That the car you mean?

Yes, it's him all right!

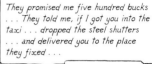

STOP!

Hands up, buddy!

You kidnapped me! Come on . . . Why?

They promised me five hundred bucks . . . They told me, if I got you into the taxi . . . dropped the steel shutters . . . and delivered you to the place they fixed . . .

What place?

The rendezvous . . . where I was to drive you? . . . OK, just to show I'm not really a crook, I'll spill the beans . . .

?

Look! A boomerang!

Thanks.

He's grabbed our bike!

'Bye, suckers!

Quick, all into the car! After him!

Here, take my gun . . .

Thanks . . .

We're approaching the city . . . Don't lose sight of him . . .

If Butch isn't on the lookout with his car, I'm a dead duck!

OK, let her go!

Saved!

A cab driven by the cops . . . hit side on by another car . . .

Say, what a mess!

Some crash!

DING DING DING

Gee! The poor kid . . .

He looks so young . . .

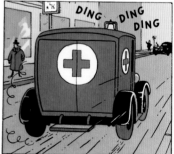

DING DING DING

Some days later . . .

HOSP

I'm glad to be back on my feet again. It could have been much worse . . .

Fresh air at last! I feel better already!

Rush hour!

What does a dog do in Chicago when he wants to cross?

?
?

CLACK

?

No one's noticed me . . .

That's that then . . . Tell the boss, will you?

Take it easy, bambino, I gotta you covered. The boss . . . he's-a coming . . .

W-w-what . . . h-h-happened? . . .

So! The famous reporter! . . . A little kid with big ideas, like he's gonna make war on Al Capone . . . On me, the King of Chicago!

You done a good job. Here's the dough.

Thanks, boss.

And that's for you. Now, just get that little squirt out of my hair, permanently!

Sure, boss.

No way to outsmart him . . . This time I'm done for!

Quick, not a moment to lose!

One . . .

Two . . .

Three!!

Thanks, Snowy! You've saved my life . . . again!

Did you see that? . . . knocked him stone cold!

Now, let's see what goes on in here . . . Maybe there's some way to nail the whole bunch of cut-throats . . .

What about letting me go for the police?

Whatta . . . whatta hit me?

I getta my own back . . . Sure as my name Pietro!

I losta my gun, but this make justa gooda weapon . . .

What are they saying?

Can you hear anything?

Holy smoke! . . . A real little tough guy! . . .
He knocked out the boss, and Pietro too!

Good, he's gone! . . . I must take
care of the other two before he
comes back . . .

Whoops! There's one . . .

. . . and now the other . . . Both securely tied
. . . The third man will be along soon . . . Ah,
I can hear him . . . he's coming back . . .

Where the heck can he
be hiding?

Watch it,
Tintin, he's
coming . . .

That puts paid to gangster number three.
Now for the police . . .

Game,
set and
match!

Quick, officer, I've just
caught Al Capone
himself and two
of his gangsters!

Sarge? . . . Send a car along. I just
picked up a nutcase . . . thinks he
captured Al Capone . . . and a
couple of his hoods.

. . . So along comes this chap and unties the others. I tried to stop him . . . But even Snowy the Champ knows when he's beaten at four to one, so I hopped it. I picked up the Tintin trail, and here we are!

You're a brave fellow, Snowy . . .

The hotel at last . . . We should have been here days ago.

Golly! It's a palace!

Ah, there you are Mr Tintin . . . We feared we weren't going to see you. But we kept your reservation . . .

Thank you, I'd have been here sooner, but I was delayed.

Aha! He's arrived. I must tell the boss right away!

You're on the thirty-seventh floor, sir.

Good.

This is your room, Mr Tintin.

Thanks.

Hello? . . . A letter for me?

Tintin:
I'm warning you one last time. There's a train to New York in the morning at 11.55. Be on it. Then take a boat to Europe. Quit Chicago by noon tomorrow, or your life won't be worth a plug nickel . . .

That, Mr Al Capone, is what I think of your threats.

Bully us, and we'll chew you to pulp!

Next day, at 11.55 am . . .

RRRING

RRRING

Hello? . . . Hello? . . . Hello? . . . Hello? . . .

Someone wanting us?

Hello . . . Hello?? . . .

So far so good! . . . He was so busy with the phone he didn't hear me coming in.

That's odd . . . they hung up. A wrong number, maybe . . . Yet someone was whispering at the other end.

Come in!

That's great work, Mr Tintin. You've captured a dangerous criminal. May I ask you to come back with us to the station? . . . Just the usual formalities . . .

With pleasure.

Please follow me, Mr Tintin, the chief is expecting you . . .

This all looks pretty fishy to me . . . Lucky I came prepared, and brought a gun . . .

Please go right in . . .

POLICE

G.S.C. . . . GANGSTERS' SYNDICATE OF CHICAGO

G.S.C.

My dear Mr Tintin, this is a pleasure! I'm glad to meet you. Do please sit down . . . Have a cigar? . . . No? . . . Then I'll come straight to the point . . .

I'm Bobby Smiles, boss of the rival gangs fighting Al Capone and his mob. I'm hiring you at $2000 a month to help me bring him down. If you rub Capone out yourself, there's a bonus of twenty grand . . . Agreed? . . . Here's your contract. Sign there.

Get your hands up, you crook! . . . And I'll take care of that paper . . . Just remember, I came to Chicago to clean the place up, not to become a gangster's stooge!

So I'll make a start by arresting you!

Oh? . . . Is that so?

Marvellous little gadget, just under my foot!

I've been tricked . . . and now I'm trapped . . . Ugh! Smoke! . . . What a peculiar smell . . . It's like . . .

Help! It's gas! . . . They mean to kill me . . . Quick, my handkerchief!

Useless! . . . I'm done for! . . . I'm choking . . . My lungs . . . they're burning . . .

There he is, Nick! . . . O.X2Z gas sure does knock 'em out!

To the waterfront, fast. Lake Michigan for him!

No one here. All clear, Nick, bring him along!

Give him a swing! . . . One . . . two . . .

Three!

That's taken care of him. Let's go!

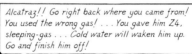

Alcatraz!! Go right back where you came from! You used the wrong gas! . . . You gave him Z4, sleeping-gas . . . Cold water will waken him up. Go and finish him off!

If you see him, don't miss, huh?

Quit worrying!

Reach for it, pals!

Lay down your guns!

Move one muscle, and I'll blow your brains out!

Thanks! . . . Much obliged, since I hadn't a gun of my own . . .

I don't wanna die!

Don't worry, I'm just calling the cops . . .

What's going on here?

Ah, could you take delivery of these two solid citizens? They're dangerous criminals . . .

Next morning . . .

CHICAGO TRIBUNE! . . . Reporter grabs gangsters! . . . Sensation! . . . Read all about it! . . . Full story! . . . Get your Chicago Tribune here!

See? . . . That's him, sitting there in the arm-chair . . . with a dog by him. Take good aim, and let him have it . . . every bullet you've got . . . And listen, fella . . . don't miss!

RAT TAT TAT TAT

You got him! . . . Terrific!

No problem. I always get my man.

How much do I owe you?

Usual fee. No extras. Thousand dollars.

Hope I've given satisfaction. Sorry I can't stay; got three more clients to take care of this morning . . . So long!

Goodbye!

How about that, Snowy? Wasn't I right to keep away from the windows? Those dummies I used are peppered with holes . . . custom-made colanders!

Dead right! . . . It strikes me . . . Wouldn't it be a good idea . . . if those dummies did the whole job, instead of us?

Now they think they've disposed of me, I'm going to arrange a little surprise for our gangster pals . . .

Using dummies again . . . I hope!

Next morning . . .

Listen, Bobby, I just heard the Coconut mob are doing a job this afternoon, running a load of whisky, hidden in gasoline drums. How's about it?

Simple! . . . We grab it!

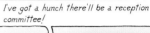

I've got a hunch there'll be a reception committee!

There! What did I tell you?

OK, come on out! Make it snappy . . . and no tricks . . .

Reach for the sky!

Hands up!! . . .

Get 'em up!!

You did a fine job, Mr Tintin . . . a fine job! Thanks to you, we've landed a really big fish, I . . .

Hey! What's that?

BANG BANG BANG

See ya, fellas!

Suffering catfish! Getting away under my very nose! And Bobby Smiles, too, the big boss!

Don't worry, I'll bring Bobby Smiles to justice!

a few days later . . .

These two telegrams are about Bobby Smiles. They say he's been seen in Redskin City, a small place near the Indian Reservations. Come on Snowy; it's Redskin City for us!

But . . . but . . . You don't really mean us to go into Indian country, do you Tintin?

Two whole days on the train! . . . Oh well, we're here at last, and that's what matters!

REDSKIN CITY

Just look, Snowy . . . A real Red Indian.

I have a feeling we look a bit out of place here, Snowy . . .

You wait here, I'm going to buy an outfit.

Redskin dogs! OK, so I'm a paleface . . . Haven't you redskins ever seen one before?

$5

$40

It's the very latest fashion . . . cartridge belt slung to the right . . . Last winter's models, all to the left . . .

Good. Just what I want!

The boss won't like this one little bit!

Boss! . . .
Boss! . . .

Boss! . . . Watch out! I just saw *Tintin* in town. I'm sure he's come looking for you! . . .

Alcatraz!!

Meanwhile . . .
Yeah! I guess I have jes' the animal for you . . .

Aha! A wonder horse!

There, she's a nice quiet gal. Name of Beatrice.

Hello, Beatrice!

Er . . . A very fine beast . . . but I . . . don't really fancy . . . the colour . . . I'd prefer . . . a chestnut . . . or a bay . . . And . . . er . . . while we're about it, have you an even quieter one?

That suit you OK?

Yes, thanks. It doesn't seem quite so . . . fresh!

Right, Snowy! Lead me to the gangster hideout!

We've arrived. I smell gangsters!

Hands up!

No one here?

Look! There he goes! . . . Escaping on a horse . . . someone must have tipped him off when I arrived in town . . .

OK, Bobby Smiles, we're right behind you!

You can't escape, my friend! I'll truss you like a turkey!

BANG BANG

Tintin! Watch out! You've roped your own horse!

Ha! ha! ha! That'll teach you to play cowboys! By the time he's managed to untangle himself I'll be far away!

Sing Sing! . . . Redskins! How do I talk myself out of this one?

How! Mighty Sachem, I come in peace!

How, Paleface! What brings white man to hunting grounds of Blackfeet?

Mighty Sachem, I come to warn you. A young white warrior is riding this way. His heart is full of hate and his tongue is forked! Beware of him, for he seeks to steal the hunting grounds of the noble Blackfeet. I have spoken! . . .

Hear me, brave Blackfeet! A young Paleface approaches. He seeks, by trickery, to steal our hunting grounds! . . . May Great Manitou fill our hearts with hate and strengthen our arms! . . . Let us raise the tomahawk against this miserable Paleface with the heart of a prairie dog!

As for Paleface-with-eyes-of-the-Moon, he has warned us of danger that hangs over our heads, and will soon come upon Blackfeet. May Great Manitou heap blessings upon him!

Now let us raise the tomahawk . . .

Big Chief him say well . . .

Pipe of peace! I can't remember where in the world we buried the hatchet when we finished our last bit of fighting . . .

Heck!

We've lost valuable time unravelling ourselves. It'll soon be dark now, Snowy, so we'd better pitch camp for the night and pick up the trail again in the morning.

We'll stop here . . .

Tomorrow morning we'll set off at sunrise . . . I'm determined that crook won't escape us again . . .

Just my luck! . . . Tintin will be here in the morning, and I'll have to skedaddle . . . They're going to find that tomahawk if it's the last thing they do!

Wakey, wakey, Snowy! On the road again!

Already?

Well, Chief?

Alas, Blackfeet still cannot find their tomahawk . . . It is lost!

What then?

What then? . . . It is quite simple: Blackfeet certainly cannot make war on Paleface. No tomahawk, no war!

Alcatraz and Sing Sing! . . . Dumb redskins won't fight . . . I've gotta get out of here!

The tomahawk!

?

Our tomahawk is found! Great Manitou wants war!

I sure hit the jackpot!

Great Manitou! Great Manitou! Give victory to your warriors!

Away! . . . To the horses! . . . Death to the Paleface!

Hello, here come the Indians . . . I tell you Snowy, if I didn't know the redskins are peaceful nowadays, I'd be feeling a lot less sure of myself!

Well, I'm scared to death!

What's all this? . . . It's an odd sort of way to welcome a stranger!

Whew! They've gone! Savages! Frightened me out of my wits!

Snowy, that was disgraceful! You abandoned Tintin.

Really, what curious customs you have!

Truly, Paleface does not have stomach of a squaw. He smiles and is calm.

But we see what he does later!

Face it Snowy . . . You've got a yellow streak. For all you know, Tintin's in danger . . .

Hear, O Paleface, the words of Great Sachem . . . You have come among Blackfoot people with heart full of trickery and hate, like a sneaking dog. But now you are tied to torture stake. You shall pay Blackfeet for your treachery by suffering long. I have spoken!

What sort of talk is that?

Now, let my young braves practise their skills upon this Paleface with his soul of a coyote! Make him suffer long before you send him to land of his forefathers!

But . . . he's crazy!

You speak well, O Sachem!

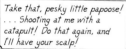

BONK

Browsing-Bison's brother, he dare to strike Big Chief Keen-eyed Mole! ... Death, I say! Death to Bull's-Eye, Browsing-Bison's brother!

Death to cowardly dogs who dare to attack Bull's-Eye because he defend his brother, Browsing-Bison, unjustly beaten by Big Chief Keen-eyed-Mole!

Splendid! Splendid! Let them fight. Meanwhile, let me get these ropes untied ...

There! That's freed my hands ... Now for my feet ... Good ... Move!

Now, who turned the Blackfeet against me? I must find that out ... What about the gangster I'm chasing? Was it him?

They've stopped yelling and shouting, so the torture must be over. I'll go and see ...

Alcatraz! ... Over there! ... He's escaping! ... Knocked out the whole tribe! ... It's impossible! ... What a kid!

Help! ... They're on my tracks!

BANG

BANG

!

I can hear shooting ... I hope nothing's happened to Tintin!

No, it isn't the Indians! It's Bobby Smiles! ... I might have known it! Now I understand why the Indians were so hostile towards me ...

Snakes! ... He's taking aim again!

BANG

?

Alcatraz! . . . What a drop! . . . The canyon goes down hundreds of feet . . . I can scarcely see the bottom . . .

Quick! Quick! I must save Tintin!

That'll teach you, smartalec! Meddling little busybody . . . I've got you out of my hair for good.

What's he looking at? . . . Surely it can't be . . . Tintin's fallen over that precipice . . . ?

And now, back to Chicago.

Wooah! . . . Wooah! . . . Wooah!

It's that dratted dog of Tintin's! . . . OK, he can follow his owner!

BANG

Wooaah! . . .

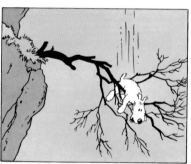

Hello, Snowy! We both seem to have come by the same route!

I fell into space, like you. It was fantastic: there was this bush, and I fell right into it. It bent and dropped me on this ledge. So here I am, safe and sound, instead of smashed to bits in the canyon.

Golly, what a stroke of luck!

Still, we're only safe for the time being . . . I can't see any possible way of escape from here . . .

What are you sniffing at there, Snowy? . . . Have you found something? . . .

Good gracious! . . . Amazing! . . . It looks like some sort of cave . . . Why don't we see if it leads anywhere?

Here goes!

Where are we?

Careful, Snowy! . . . Don't take any chances!

It's heading upwards more and more . . .

Where are we going to come out?

Look! A huge gallery, decorated with Indian paintings . . .

The Blackfeet probably hid in this cave when they were being hunted by their enemies . . .

This is the other exit . . .

Still going upwards! . . . Where can this tunnel be leading?

Ah, now it's starting to go down . . .

. . . then it's taking us up again, steeply . . .

I've got shot of that no-good reporter at last! Now, before I hit the trail again, I'll have some food . . . Too bad you're missing this, Tintin!

Hey, what goes on around here? Must be an earthquake! The ground's shaking under me . . .

?

Whew! What a weight!

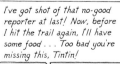

Help! Help! It's a ghost! It's Tintin!

Well, well! What a coincidence! I must say, he didn't seem terribly pleased to see me again!

How very thoughtful of him to cook me a nice little meal. I really am extremely grateful for his generosity . . . To tell the truth, I'm absolutely starving . . .

M-m-m! Me too!

Sachem! . . . Sachem! . . . I've seen a ghost! The ghost of the young Paleface! . . . He was dead. I swear it! I hit him with a bullet and he fell into the canyon . . . Now he's just risen out of the ground!

What did you say? . . . Out of the ground? . . . He must have discovered secret of our cave! Take us there, O Paleface. We must finish this young coyote!

It's about two miles . . .

By Great Manitou, I will have his scalp for my wigwam!

Paleface-with-eyes-of-the-Moon, he has stomach of a squaw!

WHEEE

Little worm . . . he escape us!

Then you'd better get after him!

Come! Let my young braves follow their Chief!

Get on with it! Faster! Faster! . . . Good grief, anyone'd think you were scared to follow your boss!

Over ten minutes since they went down. I wonder what's happening . . .

At last! There you are! . . . Well?

Great Wacondah has sent victory to his braves! Little Paleface is vanquished.

Our great Sachem did the deed. He brings his victim . . .

Fine! Fine! . . .

Yet again Big Chief Keen-eyed-Mole, he is worthy of his name. After heap big battle in darkness, with help of Great Wacondah, I, Sachem of Blackfeet, conquer the Paleface. Let my young warriors drag him from hole!

See! . . . Pestilential prairie-dog! He trouble us no more.

By Great Manitou! It is not the young Paleface!

Wriggling rattlesnakes! I made mistake! It is Lame Duck!

I have idea . . . Let us leave Little Paleface there, to starve to death in his burrow!

Do what you like, but get rid of him! This has gone on too long!

This end, heap big rock . . . other end, sheer drop! What can Paleface do? No way out but death . . .

Don't be afraid, Snowy. We aren't going to moulder away down here. They think we're trapped, but we're getting out. Look I've emptied my cartridges and collected the powder. There! Now we'll blast their rocks to blazes!

You think it'll work?

You wait here, Snowy. I'm going to lay my charge . . .

Take care you don't blow us up as well!

Done it! . . . Now . . . there'll be a tremendous explosion . . . and that rock will pop like a champagne cork . . . Any minute now, we'll be free!

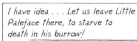

(29)

Hopeless! Not enough explosive . . . Now what? . . . I've no more ammunition . . .

Come on, Snowy, this won't do. We absolutely must get out of here . . . To work then! Let's try to dig another exit . . .

That suits me. But don't kid yourself we'll be out in five minutes . . .

That's it . . . Slowly but surely, we're making progress . . . We'll get there, Snowy, you'll see. Come on, another little effort . . . Hello, the soil feels damp . . .

You're telling me! . . . And it smells funny, too.

Great snakes! ... OIL! ... A liquid fortune, and no one to harness it!

Golly! And there's me, thinking that oil came out of a can!

OK, son! Here's the contract. Sign there! Five thousand dollars for your oil well ...

H-h-how did you know there was an oil well here? ... It's less than ten minutes since it blew ...

Know-how, sonny boy! Unerring American know-how! Never fails!

Don't listen to that crook! ... Sign here! Ten thousand dollars for your oil well! ...

Hey, buddy! Don't you sign! I'm offering twenty-five grand!

Fifty Gs!! ...

A hundred!!!

I'm terribly sorry, gentlemen, but that oil well isn't mine to sell. It belongs to the Blackfoot Indians who live in this part of the country ...

Why didn't you say that before?

Here, Hiawatha! Twenty-five dollars, and half an hour to pack your bags and quit the territory!

Has Paleface gone mad?

An hour later ...

Two hours later ...

Three hours later ...

CACTUS & PETROLEUM BANK INC.

The next morning ...

What's all the fuss?

Hey, you! Don't you know fancy dress is forbidden in town? ... And keep out of the way of the traffic! ... Where d'you think you are, anyway? ... The Wild West or something?

Out of luck again! With all that ballyhoo, Bobby Smiles managed to give us the slip . . . How can I possibly find him again now?

CHUFF CHUFF CHUFF

Here we are like a couple of hobos watching the trains go by . . .

Alcatraz! . . . I think he spotted me!

There he is!!

Station-master! Station-master! What time does the next train leave?

Next train, huh? . . . Tomorrow . . . Same time . . .

Beaten! He's defeated me again! . . . Unless . . .

Hey! . . . Look! . . Over there!

Jumping Jehosephat! My train's driving herself!

So long, folks! . . . We'll send you a nice postcard!

Terribly sorry! . . . I'm only borrowing it! . . .

Hooray! We're catching up! I can see smoke from the other train . . .

Hello? . . . Block one-five-two? . . . There's a loco running crazy on the track . . . Yes . . . She mustn't overtake the Flyer . . . Switch her on to number seven . . .

Right you are, boss! Count on me!

Phew! Just in time! Here comes the Flyer . . . with the runaway train on her tail . . .

Drat! We've been switched to another track . . .

Quick, stop the engine, and back up. We'll soon be on the right track . . .

That's torn it! The brake lever's jammed. Now I understand. This engine was in for repairs!

BLOCK 16

Only one way to clear this here track, Jem, and that's dynamite. We got plenty of time. Next train won't be coming through till tomorrow morning . . .

Sure was lucky we found this old boulder on the track, Slim. Just imagine if the Flyer was to hit it in the morning! . . . Brother, what a wreck! Fair makes my blood freeze!

Slim! . . . Train's a 'comin' . . . Quick! Light the fuse or she'll smash into the rock . . .

Help! We're done for! . . . A huge boulder on the track!

PSSHH

BOOM

Boy, that sure was close! The dynamite went up in the nick of time! Two seconds later, and she'd have been blown to glory!

Leapin' lizards, Jem! . . . The trolley with our tools and the spare sticks of dynamite . . . It's there, half a mile down the track! . . . She's done for, she's a goner!

This is our lucky day, Snowy, and no mistake . . .

DYNAMITE   DYNAMITE

BOOM

This is awful! . . . Awful!

What a disaster! What a disaster! Crew must be smashed to smithereens!

Say, Jem! This is the only piece left! Sure is grisly!

Jes' terrible!

Horrible!

HEY!

HEY! ? ?

Hey!

Where's my dog?

Your dog? Can't tell you, son. We ain't found nuttin' . . .

Pardon me, sir. Can you direct me to my wagon?

We must look! Snowy can't have vanished . . . He simply can't . . .

I've searched everywhere already . . .

Snowy! At last! There you are, my old friend! This time I really thought you'd gone for good!

You can take my word, Tintin, it hasn't been much of a picnic stuck under that coal-scuttle . . .

Hey, you plannin' on leavin'? . . . You can't light out jes' like that . . .

I'm sorry I have to go right away . . . It's important . . . I'm on the track of a dangerous outlaw . . .

Now then, off we go. With the supplies those good fellows gave us, I'm not worried about facing the desert . . .

In a small town, some miles away . . .

Yeah, that's all I know . . . When I came into the bank this morning, like I always do, there was the boss, and the safe wide open . . . I raised the alarm, and we hanged a few fellers right away . . . but the thief got clear . . .

After the robbery he got away through the window . . . Say, look at his footprints . . . a dead giveaway. See that: just one row of nails on the right boot . . .

With tracks like that, we'll soon catch him!

Madre de Dios! Thees footsteps, they geev me away pronto, pronto . . . What to do? . . .

!

Caramba! Un hombre . . . Oho! . . . Ees sleeping! . . . Bueno, bueno! . . . Pedro, he theenk he has a vairey vairey good idea! . . .

If he wake, if he move, I shoot heem . . .

Ees done! . . . Now, Pedro not have to worry any more . . .

Aaaah! . . . Up we get! Siesta's finish-ed. Come on Snowy: on our way . . .

Hello! What an extraordinary thing. These aren't my boots. They have nails, and spurs as well . . . How very peculiar . . . I can't understand it . . .

It's really quite extraordinary . . .

Look at those tracks . . . I'd say he was trying to disguise them . . . But he can't fool us . . . We'll soon catch up with him!

Extraordinary . . .

Stop!

?

OK buddy . . . You're under arrest!

!

But why? I protest! . . .

You protest, huh? . . . What about the Old West Bank? . . . And the manager? . . . And the loot?

We'll be back in town by dark . . .

They're back! . . . They're back! They got the bank-robber!

String him up! . . .

Nothing we can do, Fred . . . It's a lynch mob! . . .

Heave ho!

Go on! Laugh! . . . It could happen to anybody! . . .

Meanwhile . . .

SHERIFF

Here are yesterday's facts and figures from the City Bureau of Statistics: twenty-four banks have failed, twenty-four managers are in jail. Thirty-five babies have been kidnapped . . .

. . . forty-four hoboes have been lynched. One hundred gallons of bootlegged whisky have been seized: the District Attorney and twenty-nine policemen are in hospital . . .

Hold on, folks, we have a news flash! We just heard the notorious bandit Pedro Ramirez has been arrested while trying to cross the State line. He confessed to yesterday's robbery at the Old West Bank . . .

Well I'll be a monkey's uncle! But . . . but . . . what about the other one? . . . Feller they're lynching? . . . Must be innocent! . . .

I jes' gotta save him! . . . No one's gonna say that the Sheriff . . .

Let 'em lynch an innocent feller . . . 'Specially since I'm the only one who knows he ain't guilty . . . Aw, now, one more glass . . . Las' one . . .

Git movin', Sheriff . . . My, ain't this whisky jes' delicious . . . Now . . .

. . . One for the road! . . . Jes' to give me strength . . .

Let's go . . . to stop . . . this . . . here . . . hanging . . .

Mus'n't hang around . . . Mus' get there in time . . . hic . . . to stop them . . . hic . . . wronging the hangman . . . hic . . . no . . . hanging the wrong man . . . Ha! ha! Ain't that a joke? . . . If I get hung up . . . hic . . . he'll be strung up! . . . Hee! hee! hee! . . . That's a good one . . . hic . . .

An' I say . . . hic . . . the guilty ish innoshent . . . ish the . . . hic . . . the radio . . . No . . . ish the whisky . . . thass guilty!

VOLSTEAD ACT

WHOSOEVER SHALL BE FOUND IN A DRUNKEN STATE ... PRISON ... FINE ... CONFISCATED ... UTMOST SEVERITY ... SHERIFF

Right, are you ready?

This time, buddy, there ain't gonna be no mistakes! I got my reputation to think of...

What a dope!

Messed it up again!...

Hey, let me do it!

No!... Lemme have a go! I'll show you how!

Leave it to me!

I'm gonna hang him!

No, I am!

No, me!

No good trying to tell them I'm innocent. Better get out of here... and make it fast!

Help!... They've discovered my escape... Now they're coming after us!...

Trust Big Jim to take off on that mustang of his... Like always, he'll be the lucky guy and catch the kid!

Beats me... he's gone and disappeared some place... I know he was near this tree, last I saw of him... But I'll get him for sure, or my name ain't Big Jim!

Yipee! He went out like a light . . .

Saved! . . . They've given up the chase . . .

It's growing dark now. We'll camp here for the night, Snowy, and make a fresh start in the morning.

A puma? . . .

And a stag! . . . Since when have deer chased pumas? . . . It doesn't make sense . . .

But . . . what in the world's going on? . . .

The prairie's on fire!

Not a moment to lose! . . . Run for it! . . .

Help! The fire's gaining on us . . .

We're caught!!

Gosh, Snowy, that was close!

Phew!

I can tell you, Tintin, we were nearly beans on toast that time!

We should soon come across the railroad again . . .

You see? There it is! . . . All we have to do is follow the track to the next station . . .

Are you going to play trains again?

When we get there we must try to pick up the trail of Bobby Smiles . . .

Chuff! . . . Chuff! . . .

I'm sure it won't be easy, but we'll manage somehow . . .

Hello . . . A sleeper across the rails . . right on the bend! . . . Somebody's up to no good!

No doubt about it . . . Someone means to wreck a train! . . .

Where've I met that scent before?

Very odd . . . No one about . . .

Oh my, oh my! What a surprise! . . . Our dear friend Tintin! . . . What brings you here? . . . Looking for me, perhaps?

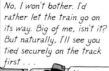
Well, well! I'm glad to have spared you a longer search . . . By the way, I was planning to wreck the Flyer . . . A cool half million bucks in the mail coach . . . But on second thoughts, I won't bother . . .

No, I won't bother. I'd rather let the train go on its way. Big of me, isn't it? But naturally, I'll see you tied securely on the track first . . .

Now . . . What's he up to?

!

Snowy! . . . Snowy! . . .

Oh, no!

Vicious little mutt . . . like his master!

Monster!

Well done, Jake . . . As you see, Mister Smartypants, he knows how to use a rope . . .

So long, pal! . . . You have just fifteen minutes . . . to think about what happens to clever little guys who try to put the skids under Bobby Smiles!

I'm done for! That fellow knows his job: these knots are like iron. Tintin, my friend, this time you're finished!

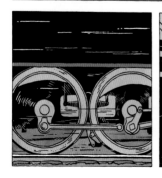

CHUFF CHUFF CHUFF CHUFF

Our dear Bobby Smiles will have quite a surprise when sees me reappear!

Oho, we're coming to the mountains . . .

Still a good fresh trail . . . quite recent.

There's a cabin up there . . . Can that be it? . . . What a superb hideout: a real eagle's nest . . .

Have we got to climb right up there?

Aha! There he is! . . . Still on my tail . . . Never mind, that suits me fine!

We don't often go climbing . . . Good practice for us, Snowy! . . .

You know, Tintin, some people do this for fun!

Wait a minute . . . He's very nearly there . . . Now for the big laugh . . .

One . . . two . . . three! . . . Up she goes! . . . And this, Tintin, is one story you won't write!

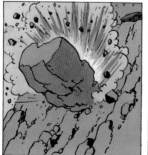

BOOM

Great snakes! He's got us! He's triggered off a rockfall . . . We're done for this time, Snowy!

I had to blow up half the mountain, but, boy, it did the trick!

Tintin, my dear departed friend, here's to you!

And to you, too!

Back from the dead!

Back from the dead, indeed! If I hadn't been protected by an overhanging rock . . .

. . . I'd be dead as a doornail!

Well, better late than never!

BANG

Nice shooting, eh, Mr Smiles?

Believe me, it's far better to give in. As you see, I always get there in the end.

Don't try any funny business!

Three days later, in Chicago . . .

Hello? . . . Yeah? . . . Chief of Police? . . . That's me! . . . Tintin? Nope! Not a squeak . . . Been gone a long while now . . . Trouble? . . . Sure is! . . . Nope . . . Ain't heard a word . . .

Come in!

RAT TAT TAT

Hello, hello! Reception? . . . This is Tintin! . . . My dog's been kidnapped . . . Yes, Snowy! Don't let anyone leave the hotel . . . What? . . . Your house detective? . . . Good . . .

What can I do? . . . What can I do? . . . If I refuse, Snowy dies! But give in to threats? Never! . . . So, what can I do? . . . What? . . . What? . . .

RAT

TAT

TAT

TAT

Come in!

You're Tintin? . . . OK . . . Someone took your dog. Ransom. You're stuck, huh? Right, ain't I? . . . Good . . . See? Nobody can fool me for one instant, no siree! . . . Let me introduce myself: Mike MacAdam, hotel detective.

H-how d'-you do?

Mind if I begin detecting?

Right, here's the picture . . . Your dog's asleep. Someone comes in. Chloro-forms the pooch. Puts him in a sack . . . the kidnapper is thirty-three years and six weeks old. Speaks English with an Eskimo accent. Smokes "Paper Dollar" cigarettes. Wears an undershirt and has matching garters . . . Easily identified by a tattoo-mark on his left shoulder-blade . . .

The kidnapper has a slight limp with the right foot; cut himself trimming a corn the day before yesterday. And one more detail: snores in his sleep . . . When I tell you, sir, his grandfather was scalped by the Sioux forty years ago, and he has a profound dislike for birdsnest soup, you know everything I've spotted from a quick look round.

?

I'll be back within the hour . . . with your dog, of course.

What powers of deduction! . . . And what assurance! . . . A real Sherlock Holmes! I really didn't think detectives like that existed, except in books!

An hour later . . .

Come in!

Hey presto! . . . Your dog!

?

Monster! . . . You! . . . You stole my little Fritzy!

47

Ouchh! The good lady certainly didn't spare the rod!

The good lady? . . . What's all this about a good lady? . . . The attacker, sir, hit me over the head with a Javanese club. It was a man, twenty-two years old, with two back teeth missing. Wears rubber-soled shoes and is a regular reader of the "Saturday Evening Post".

You're . . . sure?

Sure I'm sure! This time he won't escape me. You'll have your dog back within the hour!

Solving this case, sir, is the best job I ever did. You lost a dog? . . . One single dog?

Well, sir . . . I found you seventeen. And every one a pedigree pooch! . . .

?

Well done. Thank you very much. But we've already spent enough time getting nowhere. I think I'll continue the case myself.

Chicago Tribune! . . . New York Herald! . . . Daily News! . . .

Aha! The white handkerchief in the window . . . He's gonna pay up!

Give me a Tribune, a Times, a Herald, a News and a Globe . . . the lot!

Still nothing in the papers . . . That's good: means he hasn't called in the cops!

THE MOONSHINE CLUB

SPEAKEASY

BOOTLEGGERS TO THE WHITE HOUSE

All the same, I'm going to keep an eye on the building . . .

Careful . . . That's him coming out . . . Great Snakes! . . . Look, that parcel . . .

It's Snowy! I know it is!

He's hitting him! . . . I must do something!

If I dash round the block I can lie in wait on the corner . . .

A stick! . . . That's handy! Just what I need right now . . .

Steady . . . Cool, calm and collected . . . He's coming . . .

CLUMP
CLUMP

Oops! . . . Sorry!

Say, what's going on? . . . If I'm seen around here I'll be picked up for sure . . . Beat it, Bugsie boy!

Crikey, what a bloomer! . . . I'd better get out, and fast! . . . I'm in dead trouble if I'm caught!

BANG

BANG

THE SWORD
OF
DAMOCLES
ARMORER

50

You there! Yes you, baby-face! Come with me!

Here he is, sir! Little hoodlum!

Name and occupation?

Tintin, reporter . . .

You have to pardon me, Mr Tintin, for keeping you so long . . .

The trouble is, now I've lost track of the kidnapper . . . I'd better go back to the place I last saw him and try to pick up the trail.

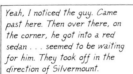

This is where I hit that poor policeman by mistake . . . Let's see, I reckon this is the way he went . . .

Excuse me, officer, but have you by any chance seen a man in a cloth cap, with a large parcel under his arm? Somewhere here, about an hour ago? . . .

Yeah, I noticed the guy. Came past here. Then over there, on the corner, he got into a red sedan . . . seemed to be waiting for him. They took off in the direction of Silvermount.

KNIGHT BRAND CANS
Come in handy!

ILVERMOUN
15 MILE

A red sedan? A red sedan just came out of those gates . . .

Could be . . .

So you got away scot free after your third job . . . That's great, great. Now, listen to this . . . I'm planning that we turn our little venture into a regular business operation. Everything legit. We'll advertise, something like: "Need a snatch? Call the experts. KID-NAP INC. Speedy, discreet, and our victims never talk . . . guaranteed. Town and country service."

Excuse me while I fetch you the byelaws of our future corporation . . .

OW!

What's going on?

Sounds as if he fell . . .

? ?

Looks like he could have had a stroke . . . Quick, go get him some water . . .

OUCH!

?

?

Bugsie! Hey, Bugsie! Wake up!

THWACK

Good work! . . . Phew! I was beginning to cook inside here . . .

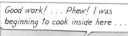

Now they're safely out of the way, I must look for Snowy . . .

At least a dozen of them after us. I can hear their footsteps already.

I don't fancy being in their clutches again . . .

Take care you don't go through the wrong door, Tintin!

KEEP

DUNGE

DUNGEONS

KEEP

He went this way . . . Look, he left the door open . . .

Dumbcluck! He's hiding in the keep . . . No way out, we've got him cornered like a rat!

Ssh! Shut your trap!

There! All gone in! Full house!

What about that, eh Snowy? . . . No one noticed the signs had been switched . . . So now we lock them all in the keep.

Nice bit of work!

Now that bunch are under lock and key, we must take care of the other three.

Half an hour! It's half an hour since they left, and not one single sound have I heard. It's positively creepy . . .

Hands up!

What the . . . ?! Tintin! . . . But what's he done with my fifteen bodyguards? . . . Still, I can't worry about them now. I must save myself!

OH!

Ha! ha! ha! Sorry I can't stay!

. . . Number one reporter Tintin triumphs again with a gang of dangerous crooks handed over to the police . . . a kidnap syndicate busted by the young sleuth. The cops also netted an important haul of confidential files. Still at large is the gang's mastermind, now the object of intense police activity . . .

The object of intense police activity! . . . Ha! ha! ha! . . . The "object" is going to show what he thinks of your activities . . . He's got another card up his sleeve! . . . Hello? . . . Maurice? . . . Yes, it's me . . . You still with Grynde?

Next morning . . .

THE DIRECTORS OF
GRYNDE
HAVE PLEASURE IN INVITING
Mr Tintin ------
------ TO VISIT
THEIR NEW PLANT

Well, well! An invitation to see the Grynde cannery. That should be extremely interesting. I think I'll go . . .

Correction! We'll go, you mean.

An economy measure to beat the depression . . . We do a deal with the auto-mobile plants. They send us scrap cars and we convert them into top-grade corned-beef cans. We reciprocate by collecting old corned-beef cans and we ship them to the car producers for reprocessing into super-sport automobiles . . .

Oh?

You see this huge machine? Here's how it works. The cattle go in here on a conveyor belt, nose to tail . . .

. . . and come out the other end as corned-beef, or sausages, or cooking-fat, or whatever. It's completely automatic . . .

Now, you keep right behind me and I'll show you how the processor works . . .

If you fell in there you'd be mashed in a trice by those enormous grinders . . . Look, down there, below you . . .

That'd be no joke!

Ha! ha! ha! ha!

TARD
EPPER
SALT
SPLATCH

Ha! ha! ha! Calls himself a reporter . . . and falls for that old gag! . . . The boss will be tickled pink!

Hello? . . . Yes . . . Ah, Maurice . . . You fixed it? . . . Good . . . Excellent! . . . What? . . . Corned-beef? . . . You're a genius! . . . How much? . . . Five thousand dollars? . . . Of course, right away . . .

Poor old Grynde! If he had the remotest idea! . . . Some of the things that go into his products . . .

What are you bunch doing, huh? . . . You guys got no work to do? . . . And who told you to stop the machines? . . . What's going on around here?

What's going on? . . . A strike, buddy, that's what! . . . The bosses cut the cash we get for bringing in the dogs and cats and rats they use to make salami . . . So no dice . . . get it?

Tintin!?! . . . Jeepers creepers! . . . A strike! . . . Surely it didn't start too soon? . . . The boss? What'll he say?

NO SMOK

Heavens, what an escape! We're all in one piece . . . If that machine hadn't stopped suddenly we'd be coming out of here in neat little cans.

I wonder how often they have that sort of accident!

Oh, my good sir! What a relief! There you are, safe and sound . . . I stopped the machine right away, but oh, how I suffered in those terrible minutes!

. . . believe me, dear Mr Tintin, I most bitterly regret this dreadful accident. You have, all too literally, had an inside view of our business . . .

I was quite carried away . . .

It looks pretty phoney to me . . . The invitation, the over-friendly manager, and then that peculiar accident . . .

A nasty piece of work, our Mr Meatball!

Yes, it's me, boss . . . We're back to where we started . . . While I was calling you a strike blew up and they stopped the machines . . . I'm afraid so . . . Alive and kicking . . . But . . . What could I do? . . . I . . .

Bungling jackass! . . . Cut the sob stuff. You don't let a chance like that slip! . . . Sure! sure! At least I'll know in future that I can't rely on you! . . . That's all . . . As for the five thousand dollars . . . forget it!

But boss . . . Don't hang up, boss . . . I . . . Hello? . . . Hello? . . . Heck! . . . He's hung up on me!

Aha! Just as well I slipped back . . . You hear some interesting things around here!

Now what's he playing at?

I'm in the doghouse!

Hello? . . . Yes? . . . You again, Maurice? . . . Now what do you want? . . . Oh? . . . Oho! . . . Good . . . That's very good! Well done. That's really great . . . I'll be there in five minutes . . . Be seeing you, Maurice!

Mr Maurice Oyle, please.

Mr Oyle is expecting you, sir.

Hello, my dear Maurice.

What? . . . Are you joking? . . . You say you didn't call? . . . You aren't playing me for a sucker, by any chance? . . . Well . . . Are you?

Golly! What a racket in there . . . Tintin's phone call did the trick!

OK! That'll teach you not to play games with me!

It's a mistake to leave your pistol lying about, my dear chap!

?

A mistake? . . . You think so? . . Not really: that gun's empty.

This is a far more effective weapon; my trusty sword-stick . . .

. . . and it's going to put a stop to your nasty habit of meddling in things that don't concern you . . . It's going to cure you . . . permanently!

CLICK

He's certainly got a point!

!!!!!

That'll nail you, Sherlock Holmes!

Just you wait, you interfering scum!... In a coupla shakes you're gonna be a pincushion!

I'm gonna skewer you!

I think he will, too!

HELP!

Crumbs! Now I'm in a real jam!

BANG

Golly! What's happening! Snowy, it's a good job you took cover!

WOOAAAAH! WOOAAAH!

?

WOOAAAAH!

Snowy! My poor Snowy!

Never mind, don't worry, it's nothing serious. You'll soon be better. After all, he might have cut your tail right off. So it's not so bad, is it?

You can talk! It's my tail, and I think it's awful! It's ruined my looks completely!

GRYNDE CORP.

Now the whole gang's safely in the bag we can take a well earned rest!

LOST BLACK CAT REWARD

LOST POODLE POPSIE REWARD

LOST SHEPHERD DOG

LOST WHITE PEDIGREE ANGORA REWARD

Help! . . .
Help! . . .

Wooah!
Wooah!

My goodness gracious!
What's happening!

No need to panic!
No need to panic!

Keep calm, please! . . .
I'm sure it's nothing
more than a blown fuse . . .

Look sir, there! . . . Someone
threw the main switch! . . .

?

It's unbelievable!
Gentlemen, Tintin
has vanished!

How disgraceful!

Hello? . . . Hello?
. . . Police? . . .
Tintin has been
kidnapped. Please
send your best
detective right
away!

Thank you for coming so quickly
. . . This is what happened . . .
Tintin, our guest of honour . . .

OK! OK! I already recognised
his dog . . .

Bring him back safe
and sound, and there's
another 5000 dollars
for you . . .

Within the hour, with
the aid of his dog,
I'll rescue Tintin and
catch the crooks!

You know something . . . it gives me the creeps out
here in the dark . . . Maybe I should . . .

C'mon Mac! Pull yourself together!
This is no time . . .

Funny
smell . . .

?

Golly! . . . It's fantastic! . . . Incredible!

Gosh, Snowy! . . . I must say, I never thought I'd see you again . . .

Tintin! Tintin!

Look out! Someone's coming . . .

Ha! ha! ha! . . . Hi! How ya doing, Mister Tintin?

You carried out my orders OK, Sam?

Yeah, boss. The dumb-bells are ready.

My clever little friend, I've got a surprise for you. We're gonna clamp this dumb-bell to your leg. Of course, it won't be all that easy to walk dragging this behind you, but then . . . ha! ha! ha! . . . you won't need to walk . . .

No! You'll need to swim! . . . Yeah! . . . Ha! ha! ha! . . . Great joke, huh? . . . See this trapdoor? . . . Down there, that's Lake Michigan . . . Get it? . . . Ha! ha! Ha! . . . Forty feet to the bottom! we're gonna see if you can swim to the surface . . . You . . . and your dumb-bell, of course!

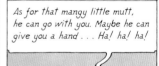

As for that mangy little mutt, he can go with you. Maybe he can give you a hand . . . Ha! ha! ha!

Goodbye, Snowy!

I won't ever leave you, Tintin!

Happy landings!

SPLOSH

And finish my report to our Association's members: I certify that in my presence Tintin the reporter was thrown into Lake Michigan with four hundred pounds weight on his feet . . . OK . . . Roll off ten thousand copies!

Hey! . . . You! . . . I recognise you! . . . You're Tintin, ain't that so? . . . Well, bad luck, feller! I have to tell you this boat is just rigged up as a police patrol, and all of us, we belong to the mob who chucked you into the lake!

Quick, Tintin, quick! . . . Hurry!

Hang on a second, Snowy, and I'll be with you!

Watch out! There'll be more of them! . . .

Let them come! . . . I'm ready and waiting!

OK, pilot, what'll it be? A quick trip to the nearest police post with you at the helm, or a brief encounter with this?

. . . And don't try to pull a fast one. I'm watching you.

You must be Billy Bolivar!

Sensational developments in the Tintin story! . . . The famous and friendly reporter reappears! Tintin, missing some days back from a banquet in his honour, led police to the hideout of the Central Syndicate of Chicago Gangsters. Apprehended were 355 suspects, and police collected hundreds of documents, expected to lead to many more arrests . . . This is a major clean-up for the city of Chicago . . . Mr Tintin admitted that the gangsters had been ruthless enemies, cruel and desperate men. More than once he nearly lost his life in the heat of his fight against crime . . . Today is his day of glory. We know that every American will wish to show his gratitude, and honour Tintin the reporter and his faithful companion Snowy, heroes who put out of action the bosses of Chicago's underworld!

LONG LIVE TINTIN & SNOWY

After a full round of celebrations, Tintin and Snowy embark for Europe . . .

Pity! . . . I was almost beginning to get used to it!

TOOOOOT

HERGÉ.

HERGÉ
★
THE ADVENTURES OF
TINTIN
★
CIGARS
OF THE
PHARAOH

EGMONT

CIGARS
OF THE
PHARAOH

This is the life, Snowy. A really quiet holiday for a change . . .

A holiday, indeed! I'd call it a deadly bore.

We'll be arriving in Port Said tomorrow. We go ashore for the day.

Then the Suez Canal, and Aden. We'll go ashore there, too.

I'd settle for Marlinspike.

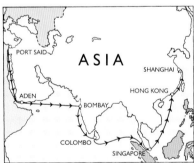

PORT SAID

ASIA

SHANGHAI

ADEN

HONG KONG

BOMBAY

COLOMBO

SINGAPORE

Bombay, Colombo, then right on round, to finish in Shanghai.

How about that for a marvellous cruise, eh, Snowy?

Marvellous . . . You mean dull as ditchwater! . . . Why doesn't someone fall overboard to brighten things up?

Stop! . . . Stop! . . . HELP!

! ?

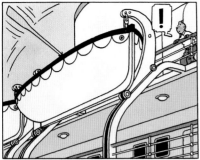

!

Excuse me, but what are you doing?

Surely you can see: I'm rowing.

But you're not in the water!

Nor I am! What an observant young man you are!

Now I wonder why I was rowing . . .

To rescue your papyrus, I expect. It blew overboard . . .

My papyrus? . . . My priceless manuscript? . . . Overboard? . . . Nonsense! I have it here.

But . . . I saw a paper blow into the sea!

What were we chasing, then?

Oh, yes . . . I remember now; it was just a travel brochure. You don't really think I'd let go of this do you? . . . My magnificent papyrus . . . the key to the lost tomb of the Pharaoh Kih-Oskh. Scores of Egyptologists have tried to find the spot . . .

Every single one has vanished! But I, Sophocles Sarcophagus, shall be the first to reveal this wonder to the world.

I hope you will . . . But tell me, what's that queer symbol?

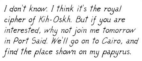

I don't know. I think it's the royal cipher of Kih-Oskh. But if you are interested, why not join me tomorrow in Port Said. We'll go on to Cairo, and find the place shown on my papyrus.

Good idea!

Till tomorrow then. Goodbye, young man.

What a strange fellow!

I beg your pardon, captain.

You clumsy nitwit! Can't you look where you're going?

So sorry, I mistook you for a ventilator . . .

Imbecile!

? Come sir, pull yourself together!

This gentleman didn't bump you on purpose.

Goodbye, everybody!

Impudent young whipper-snapper! How dare you interfere? You obviously don't know who I am.

One day you'll regret you crossed my path! Just remember: my name is Rastapopoulos!

So what? Who cares!

Rastapopoulos? . . . Rastapopoulos? Ah! I've got it: the millionaire film tycoon, king of Cosmos Pictures . . . And it's not the first time we've met . . .

That evening . . .

papyrus. Watch out! He's met a young journalist who could be a nuisance. I want him disposed of before he gets ashore.

Next morning . . .

He's gone in!

Yes, come on!

Come in!

RAT TAT TAT

You! Your name is Tintin?

Of course!

We arrest you in the name of the law!

?

70

Later, somewhere near Cairo . . .

According to the papyrus the tomb can't be far away . . .

And soon . . .

You wait for us here. We will return this evening.

Yes, effendi!

You see, a discovery of this importance must be kept absolutely secret.

Yes, of course.

You seem to know the area very well.

I don't know it at all; the papyrus gives very detailed instructions.

We're getting very close now . . .

You have a remarkable sense of direction!

If the information is right, we shall find the tomb of Kih-Oskh at this very spot . . .

What did I tell you! The tomb! I've found it! O noble Pharaoh, I have come!

Fame at last! The name of Sophocles Sarcophagus will live for ever!

WOOAH WOOAH

Hello, what does Snowy want?

A cigar . . . A cigar out here . . . How peculiar.

Good heavens! That's extraordinary! The Pharaoh's emblem on the band!

FLOR FINA

I wonder what Doctor Sarcophagus will make of that . . .

Hey! . . . What in the . . . ? He's gone!

I say, Tintin, it's just like the band of the cigar!

Where in the world can he have gone?

Yooee! Doctor Sarcophagus! Yooee!

Not a sign! He's completely disappeared . . . What was that he said? "Scores of Egyptologists have tried to find the tomb . . . Every single one has vanished!"

I smell danger: there's dirty work somewhere round here . . .

Wooah! Wooah!

Hello . . . what's up?

Aha! That explains it! Doctor Sarcophagus went inside: we'll just have to follow him . . .

Down that dark hole? . . . Brrr . . .

Come on, Snowy, careful now . . .

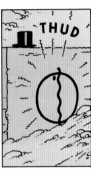

THUD

You heard that, Snowy? We're trapped in the tomb!

!

Yes, they're absolutely identical with the one I picked up outside . . .

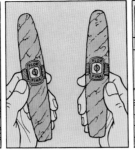

I wonder if the answer to all this lies hidden inside these cigars . . . I think I'd better take a look . . .

What . . . what's happening? . . . My head . . . I feel . . .

That smell . . . some sort of drug . . . someone's trying . . .

No! Not that!!

Meanwhile . . .

The bearded master told me to wait . . . When they did not return at nightfall I called loudly, I shouted . . . They did not answer me . . .

The next night . . .

Good. 'Sereno' is at the rendezvous. Unload the camels.

I'll flash the signal.

Ah, there's the caravan. Lower the boat right away.

Allah be with you, Mohammed . . . You've got the goods?

Yes, effendi. Everything is ready.

OK. And get a move on. The boss is worried about the coastguards . . .

Someone with a funny sense of humour, hiding the stuff in a coffin.

One of the boss's bright ideas, I expect.

Half an hour later . . .

That's the lot, skipper. All aboard.

Whew! Am I glad! Raise the anchor!

That's Allan's boat. We'll get him this time . . . the dirty smuggler!

Coastguards! Just my lousy luck! Sling the boxes overboard, fast!

SPLASH

An hour later . . .

Good thing we got rid of the evidence; they'd have nabbed me otherwise.

Message for you, skipper. It came while the cops were aboard.

Give it to me.

Three coffins shipped by mistake. They contain prisoners. Guard strictly pending fresh orders. Important. Repeat important.

That's torn it! They've been dumped! How can we find them now?

76

Not a hope of picking them up in the dark. By morning they could have drifted for miles . . .

At dawn . . .

CREAK

Snowy!

There's another coffin . . . and it's opening!

. . . ry . . . cet . . . ing . . . wo . . . ump . . . ca . . .

What? . . . What? . . . Shout louder! The wind's too strong . . . I can't hear you!

What's that? I can't hear a word! It's the wind!

. . . ous . . . al . . . ent . . .

. . . ix . . . ful . . . oo . . . ing . . . wa . . . ub . . . ite . . . re . . . ock . . .

Shout louder, I tell you!

It's hopeless. I'm just shouting myself hoarse. The currents are pulling us further and further apart. But at least you and I can stay together, Snowy. I'll tie your   boat to mine.

Now then, let's try to catch ourselves some fish for breakfast. If you're like me, you're starving.

And how!

A bite!

It's certainly a whopper!

If there's nothing else to catch in this bit of sea we'll just have to starve to death...

... or else be drowned. The wind's rising and the sea's getting rough.

Meanwhile...

It's hopeless to go on searching. We'll never find them...

Coffin to port!

Ah, I see it! Lower a boat and rescue the Ancient Mariner!

A few minutes later...

Retrieved one coffin with occupant Sophocles Sarcophagus. Weather worsening. Propose break off search.

As soon as you get a reply to that, bring it to me on the bridge.

OK skipper.

Filthy weather! And the glass is still falling. We're in for a real blow!

Signal, captain.

Secure your prisoner. If storm prevents further search abandon two other coffins and proceed to Rendezvous Three.

Good. That's more like it. We're heading south, and none too soon!

We're finished, Snowy!

Ah, he's waking up at last!

Where am I?

Now I remember . . . We were hit by a gigantic wave . . . and that was that . . .

Hello, young Sinbad! How are you? . . . Slept well?

Yes, but how in the world did I get here?

Just happened to be passing, old boy, when you were going down for the third time!

You saved my life, Captain!

Forget it . . . But I must admit I'm dying to know what you were doing, floating around the Red Sea in a coffin.

I wish I knew that myself!

Ah, here's my passenger: Senhor Oliveira da Figueira, from Lisbon.

'Morning.

Delighted, dear sir, delighted!

Allow me to assist you, sir. Any little thing you may require, sir . . . and my prices will astonish you . . .

Just let me show you, sir. Absolutely no obligation. Now observe these exquisite ties . . .

Beautiful! . . . Beautiful! . . . Look how it suits you sir . . . matches your eyes . . . Quite, quite perfect . . .

And what about a sword? Real Toledo steel!

Everything a bargain! An alarm clock? A toothbrush? A biro?

Just as well I didn't fall for his patter. You end up with all sorts of useless junk if you're not careful.

That's the Arabian coast. We're landing there.

You can carry my things over there.

You're setting up shop? . . . Here? It's the middle of nowhere. You won't get a single customer!

Wait! I haven't started advertising yet.

Hello! Hello! Salaam Aleikum! Here we are again! Senhor Oliveira da Figueira at your service . . .

. . . bringing you the wonders of the western world. Walk up, my friends, walk up, don't be shy . . . don't miss this marvellous opportunity.

It's the solo supermarket!

Roll up, roll up, lords of the desert. Act today, don't delay! Oliveira da Figueira is waiting to serve you.

What about this hat? Fit for a pharaoh! Make you the best-dressed man in the oasis!

This'll be a nice surprise for my wife!

There you are! Clean as a whistle. That's salesmanship for you! What's more, they all come back, too!

كلب ك
ى ك
!

!

Son of a mangy dog! You sold me this cake! I ate it, and now look what's happened!

But . . . but that's a cake of soap!

Before the new moon rises, by Allah, my master Sheik Patrash Pasha will have you flogged!

Next morning . . .

Let's explore, Snowy . . .

He comes!

What a quiet, empty place this is!

Patrash Pasha will be pleased!

Salaam Aleikum, most noble Sheik: the prisoner comes!

Bring him before me!

Aha! So it is you! It is you who tried to poison the servants of Patrash Pasha, infidel dog!

You mind your language!

We can do without the worthless clutter of your so-called civilisation!

What is your name?

My name? It won't mean a thing to you . . .

. . . but at home they call me Tintin.

Tintin! Can it be true? . . . Allah be praised . . . Come to my arms!

?

For years I have read of your exploits . . . Allah is good . . . that he should bring you to my humble tent!

Some hours later . . .

Goodbye, my friend. You have the finest of my horses. May you travel safely.

I will!

Goodbye, Tintin; Allah go with you!

Goodbye, and thank you noble Sheik!

Amazing what a little publicity will do for you!

Hello? I must be seeing things! A city, here?

HELP! . . . MERCY! . . . HELP! . . .

!

I can hear someone screaming . . .

HELP! . . . SAVE ME! . . .

That's a woman's voice . . .

MERCY! PITY! . . .

Brutes!

Don't be afraid . . . you've seen the last of those ruffians.

Idiot! Imbecile! Silly nitwit!

?

A whole sequence to reshoot, thanks to you!

He's absolutely ruined my entrance!

Oh heavens. I've barged in on a film company!

You deserve to be . . .

I'm sorry . . . How could I know . . . ?

What's going on here?

Sir Galahad here has wrecked my scene!

By Lucifer! Unless I'm much mistaken, you're the young man I had that little tiff with aboard the 'Isis'.

Why, it's Mr Rastapopoulos!

I'm sorry I lost my temper!

And I'm sorry if I messed up your film.

Pah! Think nothing of it! We're making a Superscope-Magnavista feature of "Arabian Knights". We've built a whole city not far from here.

I know. I saw it.

But what are you doing here, all by yourself in the middle of the desert? Come and explain . . .

Certainly . . .

An hour later . . .

. . . So there you are, Mr Rastapopoulos. That's my story. Remarkable, isn't it?

Indeed, dear boy. I find it fascinating!

I'm sorry we cannot keep you here, my friend.

You're very kind, but the captain of the dhow will be wondering where I am.

There she is, Snowy. We'll soon be back on board now.

Meanwhile . . .

Hmm . . . fresh instructions. We're to forget about Tintin, and look for gun-runners along the Arab coastline.

83

I can't see a soul on deck.

How odd, all gone . . . not so much as a whisker . . .

Sorry, I was wrong. At least puss stayed behind . . . Here, Snowy!

Wooah! Wooah!

Snowy, come here at once!

?

Great snakes! Machine-guns, under an old tarpaulin!

And rifles hidden beneath a layer of umbrellas!

I wonder where that cat went to . . .

. . . All these crates are packed with ammunition! It's like an arsenal down here!

More automatic weapons! What a fool I've been. It didn't cross my mind . . . this innocent little ship: gun-running!

Interesting, eh?

?

!

I watched you come aboard. Congratulations! I never guessed you were a policeman!

Me? But I . . .

Captain! Danger! You come quick!

If you've given me away, just remember this. My boat is mined, and I'll blow her sky high before I'll surrender!

Here, Snowy, quick! Get me out of this!

THUD THUMP BUMP

What's happening up on deck?

All quiet now. They must have made a dash for it!

In a blue funk, I'd say.

Crumbs, I . . . now I understand! They've left us alone on board a mined ship!

Take cover . . . I'm getting out of the way!

BOOM

Whew! I really thought we'd blown up . . . And all the time it must have been another boat, coming alongside with a bit of a bump.

Ssh! . . . Someone's coming . . .

At least we aren't short of weapons if it comes to a fight . . .

Aha, Tintin! . . . We meet again! . . . Drug-smuggling, gun-running, inciting to rebellion . . . You really are in trouble this time!

In trouble? . . . I wonder . . .

All right, I'll put up my hands . . .

BANG

BANG

BANG

Lights! Quick! I've got him!

Me too! I'm holding him!

He must be down here somewhere . . . We'll soon find him.

Not over this side . . .

Nor here . . .

We must stop him slipping out . . .

To be precise: we must stop slipping!

GLUB . . . GLUB . . .

Did you hear that?

Yes, it sounded quite close . . .

GLUB . . . GLUB

Sorry, I just couldn't stay under water any longer!

Saved!

Lucky for us he hooked himself . . .

Hurry up or he'll drown!

You'd better catch that animal while I take care of his master!

Stop, in the name of the law!

It's going to take more than that to catch me!

You're under arrest!

Help! Everybody out!

?

Help! He's dropped a grenade! We're going up!

Funny, something must have frightened him . . .

DANGER

Panic stations! . . . Cut the cables! . . . We're blowing up!

Goodness gracious! . . . Tintin!

Oh dear, we forgot!

What's up with them? One minute they arrest me, the next they bolt like a couple of rabbits.

A pity about Tintin . . .

Yes . . . I say, does a grenade take long to explode?

Lucky for us they ship grenades without explosive . . . otherwise we'd be sitting on a cloud by now, Snowy.

The fuse just went "phut".

TOP

Come on, Snowy, don't let's hang around here.

We'll head for the Cosmos camp. I'm sure Mr Rastapopoulos will be able to help us on our way.

There's the camp. I wonder what he will say when I tell him about our latest adventure.

My dear chap, it's exactly like a film. Anyone would think there was a plot to get rid of you!

Next morning . . .

Good luck!

Goodbye! . . . And thank you again!

Still no explosion . . .

Don't be impatient . . . Must be delayed action . . .

88

If all goes well we'll be in Abudin by tomorrow. But we must go easy on the water . . .

There aren't any wells on our way. And the desert spells death without water.

BANG   BANG

Down! Quick!   BANG

BANG

BING   PLOSH

My water-bottle!

Hoofbeats! . . . A deliberate attack? . . .

Yes, that's it: and when he saw he'd failed, whoever it was took to his heels.

He may have missed me, but he hit my water-bottle . . . and that's nearly as bad.

Many hours later . . .

An oasis, Snowy! We're in luck!

You see, one should never give up hope!

!

DANGER
MIRAGE AHEAD

Oh Snowy, I'm afraid we rejoiced too soon . . .

89

Snowy! Snowy! We're saved!

Look! This time it isn't a mirage!

A drink at last!

Hello, two Bedouin. We'll ask them for some water.

Them!

Him!

Ha!

In the name of the law . . .

Clever dick! If I hadn't listened to you we wouldn't be wearing these nightshirts . . . and then we wouldn't have tripped ourselves up!

Smart Aleck! If we hadn't been disguised as Arabs he'd never have thought we were!

We'll soon catch him up . . . he was nearly exhausted . . .

There he is!

Yes, that's him!

WHACK

!!الكن! بالله يا صحن! بانكت يبركم يي سين!

RECRUITING OFFICE

Tough nut, sir! . . . Fancies himself! Refused to enlist!

A tough nut, eh? We'll see. You must educate him, corporal!

Left . . . right . . . left . . . right . . . pick 'em up there, you horrible layabouts!

Halt! Order arms! Enough for today. Forty miles route march tomorrow. Squad, dismiss!

A rest at last!

ALI-BHAI!

ALI-BHAI!

Some poor chap in trouble . . .

You! Jump to it when I call you! Don't fool with me!

Who, me? I . . .

Four days confined to barracks! Now, clean up the colonel's office . . . And watch your step!

?

Stupid idiot! How could I forget I gave the name Ali-Bhai when I enlisted?

COLONEL FUAD COMMANDING OFFICER

?

FLOR FINA

Great snakes! The cigars of the Pharaoh! With the identical band! It's incredible!

Maybe I can find a whole box of them . . .

Got one! Hooray!

A spy! Call out the guard!

COLONEL FUAD COMMANDING OFFICER

Get moving, you men! Arrest him! Lock him up!

COLONEL COMM OFFIC

That's my luck! Just when I was getting to the bottom of the mystery . . .

Spying . . . in wartime . . . Now I really am in a jam . . .

. . . The sentence of the court is that Private Ali-Bhai be shot at dawn . . . The execution will take place tomorrow . . . The sentence will be communicated to the prisoner forthwith!

Shot! . . . I'm going to be shot . . . My poor, poor Snowy . . . This is the end!

A note . . . "Have courage: help is at hand. A friend." A friend? . . . Here? . . .

My last night on earth. Unless . . .

Tintin! . . . Tintin! . . .

?

Who . . . who are you?

Ssh! . . . Here's a file. Cut through the bars.

Hurry up! It's nearly dawn . . .

RRRZ
RRRZ
RRRZ

Done it!

Come, quick!

No time to lose!

Coming!

Free!

HALT! . . . OR I FIRE!

!

Ha! Paid off, didn't it . . . changing the time of our rounds? . . .

That's torn it. He's been recaptured!

Morning . . . It's all over . . . My last hope is gone . . .

Half an hour later . . .

Squad! Ready . . . take aim . . .

FIRE!

BANG BANG BANG BANG

TINTIN!

Tintin's dead! They've murdered Tintin!

I recognised him in spite of his disguise. Knowing the importance you attach to his disappearance, noble master, I arranged for him to be condemned to death. The execution was carried out this morning.

Wow-ow-ow! I shall never see him again. Wow-ow-oww! The only thing left for me is to stay here and die on his grave . . .

ALI-BHAI
~SPY

That night . . .

RAT TAT TAT

All is well. Everything is arranged . . . You can go there now.

Good. Here is your reward. Keep your mouth shut if you value your life . . .

A few minutes later . . .

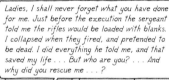

Open! Open quickly! It's the grave-digger!

All is lost! We are betrayed! The soldiers are coming! We shall be slaughtered!

That's it! . . . Break down the door!

There . . . look . . . They've escaped across the roof!

Yes, and they've taken the ladder!

Down the street! We'll catch them!

Whew . . . they've gone . . . Now then . . .

Off we go! There isn't a moment to lose!

Shuddering sheiks! It's the dead spy! Sound the alarm!

Treason! . . . Murder! . . . Kill him!

A plane! . . . If I could only . . .
No, there's a guard . . .

It's my only chance . . . I must try . . .
Help! . . . Help!

Help! Help! Save me! The dog
. . . It's gone mad . . . Stop it! . . .

Who? . . . Me?

It worked! He's
bolted! We're free!

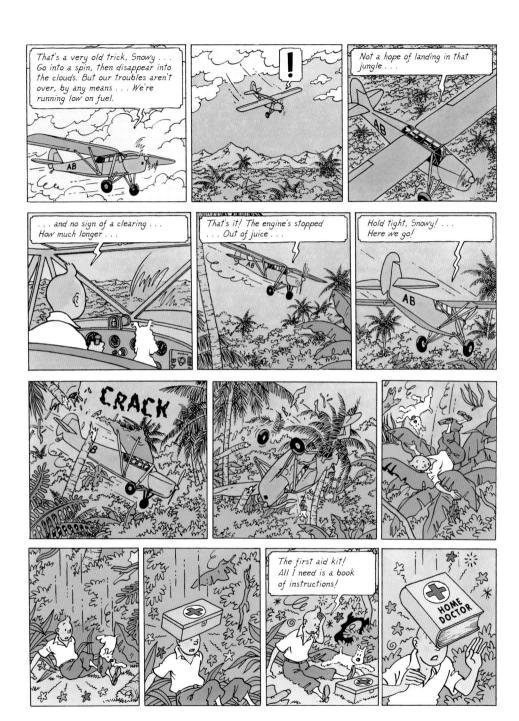

Any more to come?

Now, I wonder where we are. Somewhere in India, I'm sure, but impossible to tell exactly.

!

Don't be afraid, old chap. Snowy wouldn't hurt a fly.

Wooah! Wooah!

Good heavens, you're ill. You're running a temperature . . . Wait, I've just the thing for you.

What he needs is a good dose of quinine . . .

A whole tube. That should be enough.

There, swallow that.

A lightning cure!

Hey! Take it easy, old man!

Put me down . . . at once!

Where in the world is he taking me?

?

(100)

Look, brother elephants, this young human has cured my fever.

They seem to be having a conference. Now I can slip away.

Hrrrrm! Hrrrrm! Stop, little human. You must stay with us . . . You are our elephant doctor.

Some days later . . .

You see, Snowy, when the elephants talk to one another they make a sort of trumpeting sound. I've been listening to them . . .

I think I may be able to pick up some of their language. Perhaps I can discover what they're saying, and even talk to them. All I need is a trumpet. So that's what I'm making.

It isn't all that difficult. SOL-LAH-TE-DOH means 'yes'. DOH-TE-LAH-SOL means 'no'. 'I want a drink' goes SOL-SOL-FAH-FAH . . . Of course the main problem is to get a good accent.

Phew! I'm hot! . . . I wonder . . . Why don't I try . . .

♪♩♩♪♪

Did he understand?

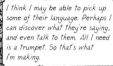

He did! He's coming back! Hooray, I've learnt to talk Elephant!

Now you stay here. I'm going for a walk.

It's time I did a bit of exploring.

!

Kih-Oskh! The symbol, here! . . . It's unbelievable!!

101

Who on earth could have painted that sign?

The ♪ sheik ♩ of ♪ Araby ♫

It can't be!

Doctor Sarcophagus!

Doctor! Hello! How in the world did you get here?

Tell me what happened . . . everything, since you floated away in the coffin . . .

Ssh! Not so loud!

I'll tell you. But you must promise to keep it a secret.

Of course . . . Now then . . .

Well, absolutely between ourselves, I'm the Pharaoh Rameses II!

Tweet, tweet! . . . Don't tell a soul . . . Nobody knows . . . I'm travelling incognito.

Poor Doctor Sarcophagus . . . He's completely mad. I shan't get anything out of him until he's cured. But where can I find a doctor?

Where? . . . Of course! That's easy!

I used to play the piano too when I was a boy . . .

What does the little human want of me?

Good day, my dear Tutankhamen.

We need special help . . . Can you take us to a village?

Look! . . . A bungalow!

Good morning. I hope we aren't disturbing you . . .

?

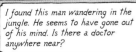

I found this man wandering in the jungle. He seems to have gone out of his mind. Is there a doctor anywhere near?

You're in luck. Dr Finney is up visiting this area. I'll send for him right away.

Look! . . . There! . . . Our sign!!

That's the whole story, doctor. Do you think the poor fellow might be cured one day?

Yes, he could . . . but he needs treatment as soon as possible. There's a special hospital not far from here; the superintendent is a friend of mine. You could take him there in the morning.

Meanwhile, you're my guest. I've just fixed a small party for tonight: do join us.

Later . . . Tintin . . . Our good padre the Reverend Peacock . . .

. . . Mr and Mrs Snowball . . .

. . . the well-known poet, Zloty.

That's a strange weapon you have there. Isn't it a Hindu dagger?

Yes, a kukri . . .

It's made of steel . . . a deadly little toy! . . . I was given it by a fakir. He told me it had magic powers . . . It's supposed to point to anyone whose life is in danger.

I'll get it down for you to see . . .

! OH!!!

I'm so sorry. I do hope you won't take it as a bad omen.

Please don't worry. It's just a coincidence . . . Anyway, I'm not scared of omens!

BANG

Don't be alarmed, it's only the wind. I think we're in for a storm.

AAAAAAH

Quick! . . . Upstairs! . . . That sounded like Doctor Sarcophagus.

Empty!! He must have gone out of the window.

HELP! . . . SAVE ME!

My wife! . . . That's my wife!

OOH!

She fainted just as I came in . . .

No one!

Oh! . . . Oh! . . . It was horrible . . . A ghost . . . I saw a ghost!

The dagger has gone! . . . Look! It was here on the table . . .

Oh, Sahib! Sahib! . . . The spirits have come for us! I saw one . . . all in white . . . running into the jungle!

First time I've heard of a spirit nipping off with a dagger! . . . Anyway, no good chasing him tonight. We'll search in the morning.

Got it! . . . A fine ghost you are!

!

My dagger . . . Boo-hoo . . . I want it . . . I want my dagger . . .

No you don't!

Shame on you, Sophocles! Be your age!

Now then, why were you trying to kill me? . . . Come on, I want an answer!

It wasn't me . . . It was the eyes . . .

The eyes? . . . What eyes?

What eyes? . . . What eyes? Ah! Now I remember . . .

Two ♪ ♪ lovely ♪ black ♪ ♪ eyes . . .

Rameses II, go back at once to the place where you saw the eyes! . . . Go!

If I follow him, maybe I can discover what this is all about.

Oh! The eyes!

Well? . . . Is Tintin dead? Speak!

No, he didn't want me to kill him . . .

Idiot!! I might have guessed . . . Never mind, I will use the poet . . . And he won't need hypnotising . . .

Hands up! . . . Fast!

You . . . I . . . Oh, the eyes!

Aha! You are in my power!

So! You cannot resist me!

Ooh, pretty little peashooter!

BANG

Whoopee! What a jolly game! Ram-Ram's playing bang-bang!

I'll shoot you, naughty thing!

BANG BANG

Whew! Thank goodness! . . . Just a butterfly.

Bang-bang all gone.

Never mind, let's go.

The fakir managed to escape . . . No use going after him . . . Let's concentrate on the poet . . . He can only mean that Zloty fellow.

A few minutes later . . .

Let's have the cards on the table, Mr Zloty. Someone's trying to murder me. And you're going to tell me precisely what you know about it . . .

Me? . . . But I don't understand . . .

You're lying! Talk, and talk fast!

Or else . . . bang!

Wait! . . . . I . . . yes . . . I . . .

I don't know very much . . . There's an international gang of drug-smugglers . . . They're determined to get rid of you . . .

And you're a member of the gang?

Yes . . . No . . . I mean . . . There is a branch of the organisation here . . . You were recognised and someone reported to the boss . . .

And who is the boss?

Just a minute . . . The boss was furious that you were still alive: he gave orders for you to be liquidated . . . Sarcophagus was to do it, while he was hypnotised . . .

But the boss . . . Tell me his name!

No . . . I can't . . . it's impossible . . . They are merciless to traitors . . . it's horrible . . .

You're going to tell me, now!

I . . . he . . . his name is . . .

!

Someone was hiding outside the shutters . . .

Too late . . . I'm done for . . . It's their revenge . . . This arrow is poisoned with Rajaijah juice, the poison of madness.

The boss . . . film . . . don't trust . . .

Quick! Quick!

Here we come ♪♪ gathering ♪♪ nuts in May . . .

Come along, children, playtime is over now . . .

Who can tell me who succeeded Rameses II?

Me, sir . . . Napoleon.

Later . . .

Now we've got two madmen on our hands.

We'll send them to hospital tomorrow.

Next morning . . .

Here's a letter for the superintendent.

Ha! ha! Off to hospital, my clever friend. With that letter they'll certainly give you a warm welcome!

109

Here's a letter from Dr Finney about these two patients.

Hmm . . . Yes . . . I see . . . Quite so . . .

Orderly, look after these gentlemen, please.

Will you come with me? . . . Just a few formalities . . .

Certainly.

There's nothing to be afraid of. They're quite harmless.

This is the sort of ward we shall use for treating your poor friends.

SLAM

?

"He will give you this letter himself. He will tell you it concerns his two companions . . .

". . . He is extremely dangerous. You should trick him into entering a cell, rather than force him. He will keep on insisting that he is absolutely sane . . ."

So, gentlemen, your unhappy friend will have all possible care.

We have complete confidence in you.

Goodbye, gentlemen.

Happy birthday, nanny!

Hello . . . yes boss. I copied the doctor's writing, and substituted another letter . . . It made out that Tintin himself was mad, not the others, and . . .

WOOAH! WOOAH!

THUMP THUMP THUMP THUMP

THUMP

37

THUMP THUMP

If you don't keep quiet we'll put you in a strait-jacket! Understand?

If this is some sort of game, doctor, it's time it stopped. It isn't me that's mad, it's the other two I brought here . . .

Just as Doctor Finney said: "He will keep on insisting that he is absolutely sane."

Mad? They think I'm mad? It's unbelievable!

Here is your soup.

My soup?

Are you joking?

That's what I think of your soup!

?

Ye-o-o-ow! . . . Ye-o-o-w!

This is it! Now or never . . .

Help! Help!

Just the wall, and I'm free!

Crikey! How can I get over that?!

?

What on earth can I do? There must be a way . . .

He'd better get a move on!

Great snakes! There they are! Come on, Tintin, use your head!

I've got an idea!

Zzzzz . . .
Zzzzz . . .

Slip under the gate, Snowy. I'll meet you outside . . .

What's he up to?

Take a good aim!

Whoops!

Cheerio!

?!

!

Whew! . . . Saved!

Now, don't let's hang around!

Stop! Stop! I order you to stop!

112

Oh no! My escape . . . cut off!

I'll have to jump for it: if I stop I'm done for! Here goes . . .

Hey, wait for me!

Confound it! He's escaped!

Wooah! Wooah!

Safe at last! Let's hope Snowy follows the railway track. I'll hop off as soon as I can.

!

Well, well, what a surprise to see your face again! We'd lost you completely!

To be precise: we'd completely lost face!

Tintin! Now I shall never see him again . . .

? ? ?

I've got him!

Me too!

Goodness gracious! It's the ticket collector!

To be precise: we've collected a ticket!

He can't have gone too far.

No, we aren't too far gone.

Hello? Jamjah . . . the station? One of our patients has escaped, jumped aboard a train heading in your direction. I'll describe him for you . . .

The train is stopping.

Someone must have pulled the communication cord.

Yes, quite a young man . . . He asked me to hide him, so I pulled the alarm. But as soon as the train stopped he ran off. He went that way . . .

SETHRU-JAMJAH

He can't have much start: we'll soon catch up with him.

Have a good time!

SETHRU-JAMJAH

This track goes on for ever. Where does it end?

Good! Someone to ask.

Excuse me, madam, I'm sorry to intrude, but can you tell me when the last train went by?

Miserable dog! Do you not know that I am a sacred cow?

You?! A sacred cow? A likely story!

You think so?! I'll teach you to mind your manners, vulgar little cur!

Where's the mongrel gone?

MOO-OW!...

Sacrilege! . . . A dog is attacking our sacred cow!

Wooah! Wooah!

Kill it!

Sacrilege! Kill it! Kill it!

We will slay it on the altar of Siva!

An hour later . . .

How can I get off the platform without a ticket? . . .

No mistake, it's him all right . . . Matches the description exactly . . .

What do they want with me?

Crumbs! Now I understand . . . My escape has been reported . . .

Hey, you! Stop!

STOP! . . .

Lucky for me I bought some bananas!

One . . .

INDIAN RAILWAYS

Two . . .

Just wait, clever-dick . . . We'll pay you back!

WAY OUT

And that's for number three . . .

ZZIP

All that, just to end up in a strait-jacket. Poor Snowy, if you could see your master now!

Meanwhile . . .

O Siva-the-destroyer, graciously accept the sacrifice I am about to offer.

The superintendent will be pleased to recover . . .

. . . this awkward customer!

. . . The patient! Where's he gone?

Quick! Look around! He can't be far away.

Free! . . . I'm free! . . .

Meanwhile . . .

Die, infidel dog!

Stay your hand, servant of Siva! The god will not accept so mean a sacrifice!

He's gone: it's all clear.

To be precise: the all clear's gone!

Quick . . . untie him.

How wrong I was. They're really pretty good chaps!

Ha ha! If we follow the dog we'll find the master.

And in the jungle . . .

By the holy brahmin! Look, Highness, look!

See! We are catching young man in tiger-trap!

I'm sorry to trouble you, but I wonder if you'd mind . . .

But of course!

It is fortunate that we happened to pass this way.

How can I thank you enough, Mr . . . Mr . . . ?

. . . The Maharaja of Gaipajama. How do you do.

Highness! Highness! See! On the branch! The lord of the jungle!

BANG

Great gods! I missed it!

GRRR GRRR GRRR

Your tiger, Highness!

?

We will return to the palace. You are my guest, Mr . . . Mr . . . ?

Tintin, reporter.

And that evening . . .

?

♪ ♫

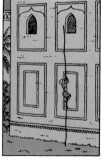

Aha! It is done . . . There goes the last of our mad maharajas!

Careful . . . he's coming . . .

What the . . . ?!

Hey, where can he have gone?

Is he hiding in the tree?

. . . In the tree!?

Oho, that sounds hollow . . .

BOM
BOM
BOM

The problem is to find out how it opens . . .

?

Got it!

A well!

Strange . . . ?!

Where does this lead to?

A door . . .

Careful! Someone's coming . . .

?

RAT
TAT
TAT

Crumbs! Another one! . . .
No time to lose!

OW!

BUMP
WHACK
THUMP

Right!

RAT
TAT
TAT

Brothers, with the exception of our leader, who is unable to come, we are all present. Our session may begin. Our brother from the West will speak first.

I have the best possible news for the Brotherhood: we are finally rid of the Maharaja of Gaipajama. Even as I speak he is going mad!

There is nothing now to prevent . . .

RRRING
RRRING
RRRING

Hello? . . . Yes, headquarters here . . . A message from Cairo? . . . What?! . . . Hold the line a moment.

Brothers, things look black. Our Cairo hideout has been raided. Only our leader escaped. He's on his way here by air . . .

Hello? . . . What? . . . Someone's just found what? . . . One of the brothers?! . . . But . . . but there are seven of us here . . .

BROTHERS, WE HAVE A SPY IN OUR MIDST!

Since our rules forbid us to uncover our faces, you will come one by one and give me our password. Whoever fails to give the word dies instantly!

· · · · · · · · · · · · · · ·
Good . . . Next!

· · · · · · · · · · · · · · ·
Right . . . Next!

I . . . I'm sorry . . . but I . . . I can't remember . . . I . . .
HA HA!

I will count up to three, my friend. If by that time you haven't given the password, I fire!
But . . . I . . . Er . . .

ONE!

TWO!

Wait! Wait! I've got it! I remember! KIH-OSKH and GAIPAJAMA!
!

Stupid fool! You're supposed to whisper! Now everybody knows!

Never mind! I am going into the next room. You will come in one by one and give me the password for our last meeting.

First!

Next!

Next!

Last one!

THWACK

Not a bad day's work! . . . I must say I was lucky to be called first . . . Now, let's have a look at the faces of our jungle Ku Klux Klan!

The fakir, a Japanese, Mr and Mrs Snowball, the colonel who sentenced me to death, and the Maharaja's secretary . . . It's fantastic!

?

Tintin! . . . Him!! . . . Here!!!

What a cheek, thinking he could tie me up . . . Me, a fully qualified fakir!

The fakir! He's escaped!

CLACK.

Great snakes! I mustn't let him get away!

BANG

Aha! Now I really have you in my power!

122

YOWK!

YEEEEK!

?

Hands up!

Snowy!!

Congratulations, my friend, you've brought off a masterly coup!

Hey! Don't you want to arrest me any more?

Certainly not. We know you are innocent. We had a call from the Cairo police. They found a gang of international drug-smugglers using the tomb of the Pharaoh Kih-Oskh. It was their secret hideout . . .

Among the papers they seized was a list of their enemies. It included you, and the Maharaja of Gaipajama. And there was a plan of this bolt-hole, too. We heard about it, so this is where we are.

To be precise: so where are we?

As for me, Tintin, I owe you my life. The dummy you put in my bed was hit by the arrow . . . the arrow intended for me.

CLACK

!

The fakir! He's given us the slip again!

Wretched fellow! He's locked us in!

Wait, I have a skeleton.

By the time we get the door open he'll be miles away. No use chasing after him. We can pick him up later on. Let's go back to the palace, and send someone to look after the rest of the prisoners.

A few minutes later . . .

Highness! Highness! The crown prince, your son! He's been kidnapped! Two men, they made off in a car . . .

Quick, the garage. They haven't got much of a start . . .

Careful, hang on tight, we're off!

VROOM

Don't fall off, you two! This is going to be rough!

There they are!

We are pursued, O Master! . . . Hurry!

The car won't go any faster.

We're gaining ground!

Smoke! What's happened?

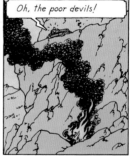

Oh, the poor devils!

They must have skidded on the corner . . .

As soon as he climbs down to have a look we jump in his car and get going!

Supposing . . . it's a trap . . . I just wonder . . .

Lucifer! He isn't going down. He'll go back to the palace, and we'll have no car . . . We'll soon stop that!

! BANG

Gangsters! A good thing I wasn't fooled!

Impossible to get him. You keep him occupied while I make a break with the kid.

Now where is he? I can't see . . .

Hands up, Houdini! And drop your gun!

There, that's better. Just a minor detail, but my gun wasn't loaded.

What a coincidence! My gun happens to be empty too. So it's just the two of us . . .

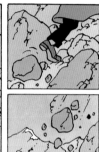

I couldn't have done it better myself!

While Snowy guards the fakir, I'll go after the mystery man . . .

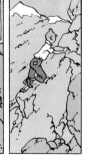

Diavolo! Can I never be rid of him? . . . But wait . . .

Come along, dear boy, just a little bit nearer . . .

HELP!!

... Missed! But I'm not finished yet ...

!!!

CRACK

?

Poor wretch. Who was he? ... I wonder if we shall ever know ... or has he taken his secret with him?

Ah, there's the prince. I must get him back to the palace.

A little later ...

My son!

Daddy!

Now, if your Highness will excuse me, I must say goodbye and start on my long journey home.

No, no, Tintin, I don't want you to go!

Allow me to insist, Tintin. You must stay for a few days at least.

Thank you, your Highness. I shall be delighted.

Hip hip hooray!

An informal shot of Messrs. Thomson and Thomson, detectives in the drug case, answering an urge call to headquarters.

A few days later . . .

Long live Rameses II!

! ! !

Play up! Play up! Now! Pass to the wing!

Hooray for Tutankhamen!

A goal! A goal! . . . Magnificent shot!

Highness, could you arrange for those two men to be brought to the palace. They need help . . .

And later that day . . .

Greetings, most noble Pharaoh!

They're still quite mad . . .

Bring cigars and a drink for our guests.

Stop! Remember, it is forbidden to touch the cigars of the Pharaoh!

?

Tell me quickly, where did you find these cigars?

They belonged to the Maharaja's former secretary. I knew he kept these hidden away. So when I couldn't find any of our usual brand, I brought these.

Just as I thought . . . The identical cigars! We found them in the tomb of Kih-Oskh . . . And the Arab colonel had some. Now let me see . . .

As I expected, they're fakes. The band, an outer covering of tobacco, and inside, opium! Quite a simple trick, but it fooled the police of half the world.

Well done, Tintin! . . . But what about our friends here?

The Rolls? Thank you, my man.

The gentlemen's conveyance is waiting.

They will be well cared for . . . And you, my young friend, have earned a good holiday. Maybe a nice quiet cruise . . . now that we have seen the last of that evil gang.

I hope you are right, Highness, I certainly hope so . . . But somehow, I wonder . . .

THE END

HERGÉ
★
THE ADVENTURES OF
TINTIN
★

THE BLUE LOTUS

EGMONT

THE BLUE LOTUS

藍蓮花

TINTIN AND SNOWY are in India, guests of the Maharaja of Gaipajama, enjoying a well-earned rest. The evil gang of international drug smugglers, encountered in *Cigars of the Pharaoh*, has been smashed and its members are behind bars. With one exception. Only the mysterious gang-leader is unaccounted for: he disappeared over a cliff.

But questions have still to be answered. What of the terrible Rajaijah juice, the 'poison of madness'? Where were the shipments of opium going, hidden in the false cigars? And who really was the master-mind behind the operation?

How can a dog get a wink of sleep? Not a minute's peace since he fell for short-wave radio!...

There it is again. That's the station I've been trying to identify...

It doesn't make any sense... What can it possibly mean?

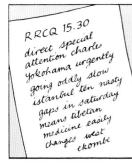

RRCQ 15.30 direct special attention charles yokohama urgently going oddly slow istanbul ten nasty gaps in saturday means tibetan medicine easily changes west ekomb

It must have some meaning ... but what?

My direction-finder shows WSW, ENE. In theory the transmitter should be along a line in the same direction, passing through Gaipajama.

Tintin Sahib, the Maharaja requests your presence.

Thank you. I'll come.

My dear Tintin . . . I've asked the famous fakir Ramacharma to demonstrate his remarkable powers.

How interesting. I'm curious to see him . . .

I'm not! . . . I remember the last one!

He's quite extraordinary!

Isn't he?

Now, if your Highness permits, I will read the secrets of the future . . .

Do so . . .

Please be seated . . .

Thanks.

EEK!

There . . . look! I sat on a cushion!

!

Forgive me . . . I have a sensitive skin!

CLAP CLAP CLAP

Now . . . Aha, I see you have a taste for adventure . . . You have already faced great dangers . . . But you are brave and . . . Oh, no! . . . The signs are not good . . .

I see an enemy! You think him dead, but he plans revenge...Be on your guard!

I also see a fakir, a disgrace to our brother-hood, dedicated to your downfall. He is close to you...very close to you. He spies upon you...He has a terrible weapon...and there is no defence.

Beware...I see another man...a man with a yellow skin...His hair is black...He wears glasses ...Take every care! He has sworn to destroy you!

Tintin sahib, there is a stranger in the gallery, asking for you. He says he has come from Shanghai to see you.

From Shanghai?

From Shanghai? That's a fair distance...just to talk to me...How peculiar.

Mr Tintin, sir?

Me? Yes...

Yellow skin ...black hair ...glasses ...Careful, Tintin!

I have something extremely important to tell you. Can we talk here?

Certainly. We're quite alone: look...

哇

?

A dart...dipped in Rajaijah juice...the poison of madness?!

He's gone... He didn't waste any time...

Quick! Speak! What have you to tell me?

I...I... Yes...I remember.

Mitsuhirato...Someone needs you...I...Shanghai ...Remember that name, Mitsuhirato...Mitsu... Mitsuhirato.

Good. Then?

TONG ♩ SI ♫ NAN ♪ PEI ♩

Poor fellow!... He's gone mad!...

TINTIN!

!

BING
BANG
BOOM

Snowy!! My poor Snowy! ... I must have shut you in the trunk! ... Well, now we can go!

Goodbye! ... Good luck!

Goodbye ...

Some time later ...

So this is Shanghai ...

That's him! That's him all right!

No mistake, that's him.

CONTINENT HOTEL

Mitsuhirato ... Mitsuhirato ... But how do we find him? ... It's certainly a Japanese name, but ...

Come in!

RAT
TAT
TAT

'TO MR TINTIN' ... Most peculiar! ... How does anyone know I'm here yet ...

Mr Tintin,
the news of your arrival fills me with joy.
I cannot convey my happiness at the prospect of gazing upon your noble and virtuous features.
May I humbly beg the privilege of calling upon you at 3 o'clock this afternoon? My servant will await your gracious reply
Mitsuhirato

Street of Tranquility

Excellent! . . . Please tell the messenger his master is too kind. He mustn't put himself out. I will call upon him myself.

I wonder how our Mr Mitsuhirato knew I was here . . . Anyway, he's certainly a man with impeccable manners . . .

Are Japanese good chaps, Tintin?

Mr Mitsuhirato, Street of Tranquillity . . .

先王！

得罪！

取清不平

取清

Dirty little Chinaman! . . . To barge into a white man!

The shots came from this direction . . .

BANG

Let's hope that whistle doesn't bring reinforcements . . .

WHEEET

WHEEEET
WHEEEET

Hurry up, boys!

WHEEEET

STOP!

!

But I keep telling you . . .

And I'm telling you, shut your trap!

Next morning . . .

Hello, Gibbons? . . . You remember your Don Quixote? . . . Yes . . . Well, I've got him! . . . Picked up last night by a patrol . . .

That's great . . . What'll you do with him? . . . What? . . . Let him go? But . . . Ah! . . . Ha! ha! ha! ha! . . . You're a pal! . . . Goodbye!

By the way . . . that little ragamuffin you brought in last night . . . Did you know he clouted one of your chums? . . . If I were you I'd give him a spot of corrective treatment . . .

Very good, sir!

CLICK CLACK

CLANG

Still, I hope they don't knock him about too much . . .

THUMP

ZZING

BANG

BOOM

Yes? . . . An ambulance? . . . To St. James Prison? . . . Right . . . I'll send one along . . .

HOST

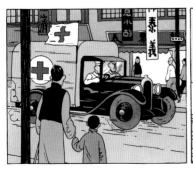

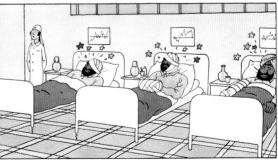

Obviously they knew I was innocent. And yet ... they didn't go after the attacker ...

A telegram for you, Mr Tintin, and a letter, and this parcel ...

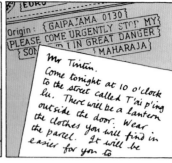

Origin: GAIPAJAMA 0130
PLEASE COME URGENTLY STOP MY SON ... IN GREAT DANGER ... MAHARAJA

Mr Tintin,
Come tonight at 10 o'clock to the street called T'ai p'ing lu. There will be a lantern outside the door. Wear the clothes you will find in the parcel. It will be easier for you to

All very mysterious ... What's going on now?

Poisoned? ... No, thank goodness! His heart's still beating ... He's asleep ... Drugged? ...

The tea! ... He must have drunk the tea I spilt on the floor ... But ... But ...

BANG

That shot ... it was providential! ... If I'd drunk the tea ...

You sleep it off, Snowy old fellow. And don't worry if I'm late back ...

T'ai p'ing lu? ...

Here we are ... Not a very healthy-looking place ...

RAT
TAT
TAT

Very odd! . . . There's no answer . . .

Oh well, I'll go in.

Nobody? . . .

Did you arrange to meet me here?

Excuse me, was it you who . . . ?

Look here, are you deaf?

Or is this some sort of joke?

OK! If you've nothing to tell me, I'm off!

Are you going to say why you brought me here?

Peculiar expression . . .

Hopeless! . . . Best thing I can do is go away . . .

Wait! . . . Don't go! . . .

I want to tell you something . . .

And not before time, too!

Lao Tzu said: 'You must find the way!' I've found it. You must find it too . . .

Er . . . yes?

So I'm going to cut off your head. Then you'll know the truth!

143

Look, you needn't be afraid. I only have to cut your head off!

He's mad!

It won't take a minute, you'll see . . .

As I suspected . . . A puncture on his neck . . . Rajaijah! . . . What can I do for the poor fellow?

Officer, I found this poor madman. Can you take care of him?

The police will look after him . . . And I'm back at square one!

Next day . . .

Mr Tintin!

Why, it's Mr Mitsuhirato!

I heard you were leaving, so I came to say goodbye. I wish you a calm and peaceful journey.

Thank you. My good wishes to you, too.

Well, I haven't learnt very much in Shanghai . . .

TOOOOT

See that young man leaning on the rail? That's him!

I see!

That night...

Are you coming Snowy? Let's take a stroll round the deck...

All right. I'll catch you up...

!

There! It's done!...You haven't used too much chloroform, have you?

Put some on another handkerchief.

PLOP

?

TOK
TOK
TOK

That's it!... Here goes!

SPLOSH

You saw? . . . They made the signal!

We'll have a look . . .

Here are the boxes . . .

There, the sampan is coming back.

The next morning . . .

What do you make of it Snowy? . . . Last night, sailing to Bombay. This morning here in this room . . .

Anyway, where exactly are we? . . .

We'll very soon find out . . .

Aha! There's someone who'll be able to tell us . . .

Excuse me, sir . . .

THE MADMAN! SHANGHAI! . . .

Have you found the way? . . . No? . . . Good! . . . Then I'll cut off your head! . . .

Again! . . .

(146)

Didi! . . . Stop that! . . .

Leave us . . . and behave!

Yes, Papa . . .

Allow me to introduce myself: Wang Chen-yee. I am the father of the poor soul you saw just now. He was attacked by our enemies and lost his mind the night he arranged to meet you in Shanghai. He was guarding you.

CRACK

BANG

So it was him!

It's quite true . . . I owe him my life. But please, why was he guarding me, and why have I been prevented from making my journey? . . .

Certainly, I owe you an apology for such a violent kidnapping. But the telegram recalling you to India was false. My son was to explain, the night you saw him, and to ask you to stay longer in Shanghai. Alas, he was unable to do so, and you set sail. But you must remain in China . . .

I must remain in China? . . . But why? . . .

Will you come with me? . . . You will understand . . .

You stay here, Snowy, and behave yourself!

Here is the friend who will be of infinite help . . .

Now Mr Tintin, it is time to give you an explanation . . .

These are the headquarters of the Sons of the Dragon. We are a secret society dedicated to the fight against opium, the terrible drug causing such havoc in our country. Our greatest adversary is a Japanese, with whom you are acquainted. He is named Mitsuhirato . . .

Mitsuhirato? . . .

Well, well! Why don't I practise on him?

What does he want with me?

147

We'll go and look in my son's room . . .

RAT TAT TAT

Didi! . . .

Come in, Father, and see an interesting experiment . . .

And never do that again!

Good to be together again, eh Snowy?

Forgive my poor son, Mr Tintin. He isn't responsible for his actions . . .

Courage, Mr Wang. I'll do all I can to find an antidote to that terrible poison . . .

Now, when Mitsuhirato had failed to stop you coming to China, he tried to scare you into leaving immediately. When you stayed, he tried to kill you. Now he believes you are on the way back to India. So far so good. We know he communicates by radio with his accomplices . . .

By radio? . . . Well, well . . . What a pity my receiving set is in my trunk aboard the 'Ranchi' . . . I could have . . .

Your trunk came with you, dear friend. We would not wish to deprive you of your luggage . . .

Look . . . One day in Gaipajama I intercepted this peculiar message: 'Direct special attention Charles Yokohama urgently going oddly slow Istanbul ten nasty gaps in Saturday means Tibetan medicine easily changes West Ekombe'. I couldn't make head or tail of it . . .

Then, on my journey, I managed to solve it. Take the first two letters of each word, and that gives you: 'Dispatch your goods. Listen again same time each week.'

The word Yokohama made me think the sender of the message was Japanese and . . . Wait! A signal on the same wavelength . . .

blizzard
ueda
location
tuesday
storm
entraps
top nine
ghurkas
T

Take the first two letters of each word . . . there . . . 'Blue Lotus ten tonight' . . . Well, that doesn't make much more sense . . .

Blue lotus . . . Blue lotus . . . Wait . . . Yes, I know . . . . In Shanghai there's an opium den with that name . . .

An opium den? Right! I'll be there tonight . . .

That night, at ten o'clock . . .

蓮

THE BLUE LOTUS

No, Mr Mitsuhirato has not yet arrived. But he won't be long. Please come with me.

I'll wait for him here . . .

Good evening, sir. Someone is waiting for you . . .

Yes, I know.

Here are 5000 dollars in advance. You get the same again when the job is done. But just remember, if you talk . . . you die! . . . You understand? . . . Good! . . . Now, we go.

Good night, master.

Get in . . .

You have everything?

Careful! . . . We've arrived . . .

Now then, to work! . . .

Crumbs, it's cold . . . Now what are they doing? . . . Taking cover? . . . I wonder . . .

Perfect!

Hello? . . . Cheng Fu station? . . . Chinese bandits have just blown the track . . . At post 123.

Brrrr! I'm frozen!

ATCHOOOO!

!   ?

Someone over there! . . . Look! . . . A spy! . . .

BANG

Tintin should have been back long ago...

Where in the world can he be?

My driver will take you back to Shanghai...I have unfinished business with our young friend!

They've brought me here and locked me in... What will they do next?

My dear Mr Tintin, do forgive me for not paying attention to you sooner...

Well, what are you going to do with me?

I'm going to enjoy myself, dear friend. Here on the outskirts of Shanghai no one saw you arrive, and no one will ever see you leave, if that's what I decide.

You are at my mercy. If I so wish, you will vanish!...But all things considered, I don't want to kill you. No, on the contrary. I've decided to let you go...

!

Excuse me...I'll be back in a moment...

I...of course... As you wish...

I must say, I hadn't expected this...

Do you know what this is?...

The poison of madness!!!

Just one little jab... and I'll set you free...

Don't be afraid! ...Only a little dose...We don't want to over-do things!

There!...You see... It didn't take long...

Mad!... I'm going to go mad!

And Chang?... He's still not back either?

No, Venerable, not yet.

Whatever happens, I simply must find Tintin!...

Each ♪ peach ♪ pear ♪ plum ♫ In comes ♪♪ Tom ♪♪ Thumb! ... ♪♪♪

And now, my little man, out you go!

Chick...chick... chick...chicken!

Yip-I-addy-I-ay! . . .

Goodbye! Have a good time!

Happy days are here again! . . .

He still isn't back . . .

TINTIN!

Wooah! Wooah!

♪ Tarantara ♫ zing boom Zing ♪ boom ♪ boom

Golly! . . . He's . . . Tintin's . . . drunk!

BRRRRRRRRRR . . . Look out! . . . I'm coming in to land!

Or else he's mad!

Too-ra ♪ loor-ra loor-ra-lay ♫

My dear old Snowy! Did you think I'd gone crazy?

Still, I wonder why I haven't? . . . He very definitely stuck a needle in my arm . . .

Seven suffering Samurais! That's not Rajaijah... So what did I ...?

Chang went to watch the house of Mitsuhirato, Venerable... He has returned...

Send him here at once!

I was hidden in the next room. I put coloured water in place of the Rajaijah, and I've brought you the real poison. I took care of his knife and his gun too...

I'll soon find him. He can't have gone far...

There!! ...

CLICK

?

I could have sworn my gun was loaded ... Anyway, I still have my knife!...

Kamikaze! The blade's made of rubber!

!

!

And perhaps that's made of rubber as well! ...

An hour later ...

Major, I'm Japanese... I've been half murdered by a young European, a Chinese spy! His name is Tintin!

Now we must go back to Mr Wang ...

5000 YEN REWARD

TINTIN SPY

!

There isn't a moment to lose ... I must get out of the city ...

Too late! Japanese patrols are watching the gates. I can't get past! . . .

How to escape from the city? . . .

?

You're the one with a Japanese price on your head!

Hide yourself! Quick!

Hello? ...Yes? ... Still not found him? ...Then search harder! ...How could he have passed the city gates?

Thanks!

You saved my life. I shall never forget . . .

Don't thank me . . . My brother is a rickshaw boy. You rescued him from a foreign devil.

A real friend!

Blow me, if that isn't Tintin! . . . Stopped me teaching manners to that Chinese chimpanzee!

What's he doing out here, dressed like a native? . . . Very fishy! . . . If I'd seen him sooner I'd have knocked him flat!

5000 YEN
REWARD
TINTIN
SPY

Take me to your officer! . . . I know where Tintin is, see?

So? . . . You are sure of your facts?

Absolutely certain, Major . . . I saw him clearly as I'm seeing you!

If we walk fast we'll be back with Mr Wang by tonight.

?

Lucky for me I was hidden. I'd better keep an eye open in case he returns . . .

Careful! Here comes that armoured car again!

We didn't find him, sir. Not a chance of his escaping along that road . . .

(158)

At last! . . . I thought I'd never see you again!

You lied! . . . We found no trace of Tintin . . . You will be detained . . . And mark my words: no one plays the fool with the military authority! . . .

But . . . but . . . I . . . .

Just let me get out of here and I'll show him what I'm made of, the little swine!

So this is the mysterious poison that's done so much damage . . . and if it hadn't been for your servant I'd have been a victim, too . . .

AYAYAH! OHO! YOUP!

? ?

Our son is having another fit of madness, Wang. Please, try to calm him!

YAAH HI

Poor, poor Mrs Wang . . .

If only someone could do something to cure his madness, but that's impossible . . .

Unless . . . yes, but it's only a chance in a million . . .

And if I do that, I'll have to get back through the Japanese lines . . .

Don't cry, Mrs Wang . . . Tomorrow morning I'll go to Shanghai and I'll have that poison analysed. Who knows, perhaps we may find a cure for your son's madness.

Next morning . . .

I fear for you. Don't forget there is a price on your head!

Don't be afraid . . . If I can manage to reach the International Settlement, I'll be safe. They can't do anything to me there . . .

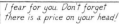

Hello? . . . Yes, speaking . . . To whom have I the honour . . .

Dawson here, Chief of Police of the International Settlement . . . I believe you're holding a chap called Gibbons . . . Yes . . . From a large American company . . . I think you'd be wise to let him go . . . Could make an awful lot of trouble . . .

Agreed, but on one condition . . . We're looking for a spy, name of Tintin. If he takes refuge in the International Settlement, you'll hand him over . . .

It's a deal, Major . . . You can count on me!

You've really made up your mind, then?

Yes. But don't worry. All will be well . . . And I'll keep in touch with you . . .

Now, how am I going to get myself into the city?

I tell you, Tintin, it's absolutely crazy! . . .

What? . . . Still not caught him? . . . Seventy suffering Samurais! . . . Very well, double the reward! Ten thousand yen for his capture!

There's a new general coming here this morning on a tour of inspection. I want everything in perfect order . . . Turnout, barracks, the lot!

Present arms!

? Yes, General, I haven't had time to shave this morning.

Four days' detention?!! . . . I . . . very good, sir!

The paper? . . . It just blew here, General . . . Very sorry, sir.

?

Four days' detention!?! . . . But sir, it's only a piece of paper . . .

Eight days?!! . . . I . . . Very good, sir!

 Full of charm, isn't he? And that's our new general!

Major, there's a little man who insists upon seeing you. He claims to be the general.

 Bring him in. I'll give him general!

 But... but the general has just left!

And I'm telling you, blockhead, that I'M General Haranochi! ... I was attacked on the road by a young Chinese who stripped me of my uniform!! ...

 No one about? ... Good!

 Here we go! ...

 One ...

Two ...

And three!

 Now let's release my false stomach ... All right, Snowy?

 Now to the International Settlement ... And make it snappy!

 All's well. We made it!

 Halt! ... Your papers!

 My identity papers? ... I'm afraid I haven't got them with me ... But my name's Tintin and I ...

Sorry! ... Nothing doing!

 But look! You can see I'm a European ...

Nothing doing!

 What's the problem?

The boy hasn't any papers, sir ...

Please ...

 No use arguing, sonny. Must have proper papers to enter the Settlement ...

 Now what? ... Crumbs! A Japanese patrol! I must get in. If I don't ...

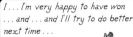

* See Cigars of the Pharaoh

Is Professor Fang Hsi-ying at home please?

Honourable master has not yet returned. But he will not be long. Will you wait?

My heart is anxious. Honourable master told me he would be home by ten o'clock. Now it is after midnight . . .

Do you know where he went?

Yes, he went to a reception given in his honour by his friend Mr Liu Ju-lin in the Street of the Purple Mountain.

Then I'll go there . . .

What? My honourable friend has not reached home? . . . Strange . . . He left at about ten o'clock with one of our guests, Mr Rastapopoulos.

Rastapopoulos, here? . . . Where is he staying?

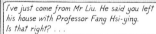

The Palace Hotel, quick! . . .

Come in!

RAT TAT TAT

Good evening, Mr Rastapopoulos!

Tintin! What a pleasant surprise! . . .

I've just come from Mr Liu. He said you left his house with Professor Fang Hsi-ying. Is that right? . . .

Yes, quite right. I gave the professor a lift in my car and left him at the corner of the Street of Infinite Wisdom, where he lives . . . Why do you ask?

Professor Fang Hsi-ying never got home.

Didn't get home? . . . But it's only a few steps to his door from the place where I dropped him . . .

Hello? . . . Yes, it's me . . . What is it? . . . What?!! You didn't arrest him? . . . Dozy dolt!

It wasn't my fault, Chief. The porter didn't warn me soon enough. He'd already gone . . .

Next morning . . .

Your master still hasn't come home? . . . Very odd . . . Well, I'll see what I can do . . .

Thank you!

Let's go over the professor's route from the time he got out of Rastapopoulos's car . . .

Aha! A patch of oil . . . A car must have parked here. I'm certain someone was waiting for the professor and grabbed him . . .

OH!

Wooah!

W.R. GIBBONS
Director

AMERICAN & CHINESE STEEL INCORPORATED

NEW YORK   SHANGHAI

53, Bund   Shanghai

Gibbons . . . I don't know that name.

He didn't wish to give his name, sir, but he told me he'd only be a minute . . .

OK. Let him in . . .

Please come in . . .

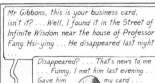

Mr Gibbons, this is your business card, isn't it? . . . Well, I found it in the Street of Infinite Wisdom near the house of Professor Fang Hsi-ying . . . He disappeared last night . . .

Disappeared? . . . That's news to me . . . Funny, I met him last evening . . . Gave him my card . . .

He seemed worried . . .

Street of Infinite Wisdom . . . Fang Hsi-ying . . .

Hello! . . . Hello! . . . Get me the Chief of Police! Fast!

Hello? . . . Richards? Take Brown and go to the Fang Hsi-ying house on the Street of Infinite Wisdom. Tintin is on his way there. Handcuff him and bring him here!

Fang Hsi-ying's house! . . . At the double! . . .

Oh, it is you, sir! ... Come, please! ... I have just received a letter from Honourable Master!

A letter?

Dear Chen,
I have been seized by Chinese gangsters demanding a ransom of 50,000 dollars. It is essential the police do not look for them. If they are alarmed they will kill me.
The ransom is to be left, within a fortnight, at the old temple about an hour's journey from Hukow on the right bank of the Yangtze Kiang. As I do not possess sufficient money

I'm going to look for the Professor ... While I'm gone will you look after this package? ... Please, take the greatest care of it ...

OK, Chief, we got Tintin for you.

Well done, Richard's ... Bring him in ...

I'd like to know why you've arrested me ...

Just a second, old man, and you'll be in the picture ...

Hello? ... Japanese border post? ... Is that you, Major? ... Dawson here ...

Yes ... yes ... Tintin! ... You arrested him? ... Congratulations! ... Yes, that's right ... Excellent ... In half an hour ... Goodbye ...

It's disgraceful! ... I'm on international territory here and you have no right to hand me over to the Japanese! ...

Excuse me, you're quite wrong ... Have you papers allowing you to be in the Settlement? ... No, you haven't ... So I have the right to expel you ... If the Japanese arrest you, that's none of my business ...

Half an hour later ...

Hello . . . yes . . . Tintin! . . . You got him? . . . His trial begins tomorrow? . . . How long will it last? . . . Two days? . . . Good!

Two days later . . .

Venerable Master, Tintin is a prisoner of the Japanese and they've condemned him to death! . . . I saw posters in the city! . . .

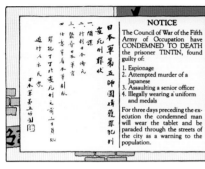

NOTICE

The Council of War of the Fifth Army of Occupation have CONDEMNED TO DEATH the prisoner TINTIN, found guilty of:

1. Espionage
2. Attempted murder of a Japanese
3. Assaulting a senior officer
4. Illegally wearing a uniform and medals

For three days preceding the execution the condemned man will wear the tablet and be paraded through the streets of the city as a warning to the population.

Three days go by . . .

Tomorrow at dawn Tintin ends his career . . . I can't see any way to get myself out of this one . . .

You really think he'll accept? . . . Seriously?

Now what do they want?

Hello, dear friend . . .

Mitsuhirato!

I come to you as a friend, dear Tintin . . . No, no I'm not joking. I've come to offer you your freedom!

Really?

Yes, but on two conditions. First, that you join our counter-espionage service. Second, that you tell me where you've hidden the poison you stole . . .

That's all?

That's all. Here are 10,000 dollars. You accept my proposition, I get you out tonight, and the money's yours . . .

He refused? . . .

How did you guess?

168

It's Mr Wang! . . .

How can I thank you?

Ssh! Not a sound! . . . We must hurry! . . . Follow me, quickly!

I'll lead the way . . .

Are you following me?

Yes, I'm behind you, Mr Wang.

There! . . . Now you're in my house!

Your house?

My house, yes . . . It's the one next to where you were imprisoned. As soon as I heard you'd been sentenced I rented this house. Then I made use of the three days you were being paraded to dig this tunnel . . .

We must leave the city at once. It will soon be light and the alarm will be raised . . . Ah, is everything ready?

Yes . . .

Vanished? The prisoner vanished? . . . Blockhead! . . . When you're guarding a prisoner you don't let him escape . . . And the major? . . . What's the major going to say?

Escaped? . . . Bungling blockheads! . . . When you're guarding a prisoner you watch him! . . . And the general? . . . What's the general going to say?

Blockheaded bungler! . . . When you're guarding important prisoners you're on your guard! . . . Now don't let this news get out!

Flaming Fujiyama! Tintin has escaped!

Double the guard on the gates . . . He can't be allowed to get out of the city. We'd be a laughing-stock! . . .

My brother told me, and he had it from one of the guards. Young Tintin escaped from prison, right under their noses!

Ah, so! That pest Tintin has escaped . . . I've got to keep my eyes open.

Wait! . . . What's inside those sacks?

It's rice, Lieutenant.

We'll see about that! Run your bayonet through each sack!

All done, Lieutenant!

You can go!

Have you seen a cart go past with sacks on it, pushed by three Chinese?

Yes, I saw it. Why?

They've made a fool of you, Lieutenant! . . . Tintin was hidden in one of those sacks!

!

Now I'm in trouble! . . . But I don't understand . . . We bayonetted every sack . . .

Sergeant-major, the sentry guarding the armoured cars has disappeared.

I'm going tomorrow to Hukow, on the Yangtze Kiang. That's where the ransom for the professor is to be paid to the kidnappers.

The next morning...

Didn't you know?... The river has broken its banks... Everyone is fleeing from the floods.... I doubt whether you will be able to reach Hukow at all...

What is happening?

The train isn't going any further. The line is cut...

Is it far to Hukow?

Three hours on foot...

Help! Help! Help!

What an excellent idea! . . . It remains to be seen if the Chief of Police will agree . . .

Oh, I can vouch for him, General . . . Look . . .

9, J. M. Dawson, Chief of Police of the International Settlement, owe the sum of 10,700 dollars to Mr Mitsuhirato.
J. M. Dawson
Shanghai   18. X. 31

He! he! Marvellous!

Next day . . .

Mr Mitsuhirato? . . . Very well, show him in . . .

Good morning, Mr Mitsuhirato. What fair wind blows you here?

I come to beg a favour . . . If you agree to grant it, then in return I'll forget all about that trifling sum of money you owe me . . .

What are you getting at?

Quite simply . . . Tintin is now in Hukow . . . And I want you to get him arrested . . .

Hukow? . . . That's Chinese territory. My jurisdiction is limited to the International Settlement . . .

Of course, but the Chinese wouldn't refuse you permission to go after a European, even outside the Settlement . . .

No, maybe not . . . But what reason can I give? . . . Tintin hasn't committed any crime . . .

A reason? . . . How should I know? . . . What if you suspect him of involvement in the kidnapping of Professor Fang Hsi-ying, for example . . .

That's an idea . . .

Chinese Police Head-quarters . . . Good morning, Mr Dawson . . . What? . . . Fang Hsi-ying? . . . You've got a lead? . . . A European? And you want a pass for your detectives . . . Of course . . .

That's it . . . We'll have the pass tomorrow morning. My men will leave as soon as it comes.

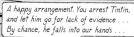

A happy arrangement. You arrest Tintin, and let him go for lack of evidence . . . By chance, he falls into our hands . . .

Right . . . and you cancel that trifling debt of mine . . .

Hukow . . .

My father had a friend in the town . . . We'll ask if we can stay with him . . .

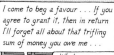

Of course . . . What greater happiness! My friend's son under my humble roof . . .

You already have travel permits. This is a safe-conduct from the Chinese authorities. It will facilitate your mission . . .

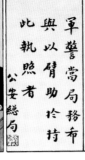

此執照者 公安總局 與以臂助於持 軍警當局務希

POLICE HEADQUARTERS

All Chinese authorities are hereby direct-ed to render whatever as-sistance may be required by the bearer of this pass.

A rotten job!

Just our luck! . . . Ordered to arrest a friend!

There's a train later this evening. That gives us time to get ourselves ready . . .

Next morning . . .

What a life . . . All night in the train . . . then three hours' walk . . . Hukow at last . . .

Just as well we came in disguise . . .

Precisely!

Imagine the sensation we'd have caused, coming to a place like this in European clothes . . .

!

Don't look now, but something tells me we're being followed . . .

Hey!! . . .

Goodness! . . . Gracious! . . .

Hello, what brings you here?

Poor soul, if only you knew . . . How to tell him? . . .

Come on, then . . . What's the matter?

Look at this.

A warrant for my arrest! . . .

And this . . . All Chinese authorities have to render assistance to the bearer of this pass . . .

All right, do what you must. I'm ready to go with you . . .

Goodbye, Chang. I'm being arrested. I have to go with them . . .

Now for the Chief of Police!

We've just arrested this young man, Your Honour. Here is our authorisation to operate in Chinese territory . . . Oh dear! Where's it gone?

Into the other pocket, obviously!

Goodness gracious! It isn't there either! . . . What . . .

I can't have put it away properly . . . I showed it to the prisoner . . .

Well, where is it?

What luck! . . . There it is!

Here it is! I found it!

(176)

Of course! I should have realised immediately.

What's so funny, Your Worship?

To be precise, why's he making fun of us?

You're funny, all right! ...Ha! ha! ha! Here, you can have your precious paper... Then you'd better get out, fast! ...Without your prisoner!

It's disgraceful! We're a disgrace!...

It's...it's monstrous!

You'll hear more of this, Monstrosity!

We must do something!

We need something to do! Shanghai must be told!

As for you, young man, you're free to go, of course.

Thank you very much, Superintendent.

Here I am!

Free?

Yes, free...but I can't imagine why... The Superintendent took one look at the paper, roared with laughter, and threw the detectives out!... It's extraordinary, don't you think?

Not really. You see, I wrote the paper they showed to the Superintendent...it was like this... The real document...

...fell to the ground. I picked it up, and ran to the house. I found some paper just the same, and wrote: 'In case you haven't noticed, we are lunatics and this proves it.' Then I put my paper in place of the other one...

Now I understand!... What a good friend you are, Chang!

Poor Thomson and Thompson!

Don't worry Tintin... They deserved it.

Kindly send this telegram to the Chief of Police, International Settlement, Shanghai...

Now we must look for Professor Fang Hsi-ying...

Yes, but there's a storm coming...

Botheration! Telegraph lines to Shanghai are cut because of the floods. We'll have to go ourselves . . .

To be precise . . . Shanghai will be flooded with telegrams because we cut ourselves . . .

Here's the storm . . . I think we'd be safer to go back down . . .

You're right, Chang . . .

Meanwhile, in Hukow . . .

Here's my messenger! . . . You've got news of Tintin's arrest, that's for sure!

'Arrest failed. Tintin free. Instructions awaited.' Seventy-seven suffering Samurais!

I want this finished! Desperate cases call for desperate remedies! 'Liquidate!' One word, that's enough!

What a beastly business . . . travelling all night . . .

All because of that rotten commissar! . . .

The next morning . . .

That's the old temple they mean . . .

A lot of tourists must visit this old temple. Look, Chang, there's even a photographer . . .

Picture of you together, gentlemen? Ready in five minutes . . .

OK? If you like . . .

Ready now . . . Watch the birdie! . . .

BANG
BANG BANG
BANG

Infernal machine! My tommy-gun jammed! . . .

Filthy Chinese! . . . I'll teach you to mind your own business!

Hands up, gangster, or I'll 'photograph' you at point blank range!

Now then, start talking! Japanese, aren't you? . . . Mitsuhirato put you up to this, didn't he?

Yes, he's afraid of you . . . You have the Rajaijah poison. If you find Fang Hsi-ying, he thinks the professor will develop an antidote . . . That's why he kidnapped the professor . . .

So that was him, too! What about the letter accusing Chinese gangsters?

The ransom letter was a fake to lead the police on a false trail.

A fake! I should have guessed it!

So Professor Fang Hsi-ying is not in the old Temple . . . Where is he?

I don't know.

That's a lie!

It's the truth! I swear! . . . Only Mitsuhirato knows where the professor is . . .

All right, we'll go back down to Hukow . . . Nothing serious, is it, Chang?

No, luckily the bullet only grazed your shoulder.

The Chinese police can handle this thug . . .

That's put him behind bars . . . Now, Chang, if Mitsuhirato won't come to us, we'll go to Mitsuhirato! . . . What do you think?

I agree!

All right, off we go to Shanghai!

That's the Shanghai train coming now . . .

Here we are again.

To be precise: here we aren't. It's three hours, walk to Hukow . . . What a life, Thomson, what a life!

I was behind him . . . I saw him trip over the suitcase and fall on the platform. Just a silly accident.

Ah! He's beginning to come round . . .

TINTIN!

What about Tintin? . . . On the platform! . . . Waiting for the train!

The train! It's leaving for Shanghai . . .

Great snakes! Thomson! . . . Let's hope he doesn't catch us! . . .

. . . I was just catching it, but I didn't notice I'd run out of platform! . . .

Only one thing to do: warn Shanghai by telegram. They'll arrest him on arrival . . .

Why shouldn't he be? ... He's been there for over a week ...

You're right, Yamato, it's just that I'm itching to get my hands on the lot of them!

All clear: you can come ...

What's the matter? ... You seem worried ...

I'll explain later, Chang ... Hurry! We haven't a moment to lose ...

A car, quickly! We need a car!

At last ... there's one now ...

Quick, driver, quick! ... Take us to the Nanking road!

Look here, I'm not a taxi! ... Can't you see this is a private car?

!

Doesn't matter! For heaven's sake get going! ... Please! ... Lives are at stake!

No, no, no! ... And when I say no I mean no!

They know everything, I heard them ... They know Mr Wang has been looking after us ... They're going to kidnap him tonight with his wife and son ... And us too, if they find us there ...

Shall we be in time?

All seems quiet . . .

The door isn't closed! . . .

It's Mr Wang's servant! . . . He's been chloroformed! . . .

Too late! They've been kidnapped!

The game's up, Mr Wang! . . . You are all in my power! . . . There's only Tintin . . . In a few hours he too will have ceased to annoy me! . . .

Tintin! . . .

Look what I've found . . .

Blue Lotus Wang.

Come on!

To the Blue Lotus!

The Blue Lotus? . . . It's an opium den in Shanghai . . . How do I get in without being recognised? . . . In disguise? . . .

Will there be anything more, sir?

No, no thank you . . .

He is here . . .

You're sure it's him?

Indeed, Master . . . He has tried to disguise himself . . . A fake beard and a black wig, but I recognised him . . .

Now for some fun! . . .

WHEEET

Oh, my goodness! Someone seems to have a bone to pick with me!

BANG

That's it! . . . Let him have it!

OH!

THUMP

BANG

YEOW

Not a bad idea, was it, my friend? . . . That trick with the little bit of paper, with a scrawl on it by Mr Wang . . .

184

I protest! . . . I . . . I protest! . . .

He! He! You protest! . . . You've got a nerve, I must say!

OW! . . .

YEOW!

Fujiyama! . . . Not Tintin! . . . Untie him! . . .

No, I am not Tintin! I am the Consul for Poldavia! . . . You'll hear more of this, villain!

Forgive me, sir, it was all a mistake . . . I took you for somebody else . . .

Even for somebody else, that's no way to treat people! . . . You will pay dearly for this!

Seven hundred suffering Samurais! . . . Wait till I get him, just wait till I get him!

I'm going home! . . . Yamato, be ready with the lorry at midnight tomorrow, at godown No. 9. The 'Harika Maru' will moor alongside. Load the goods and take them to the warehouse . . .

Yes, Master . . .

Goodbye! . . . Telephone me if there are any developments . . .

Right, Master . . .

I don't think Tintin will come . . .

No, he'll be suspicious . . .

Ha! ha! None of that fell on deaf ears! . . .

THE BLUE LOTUS

Any news?

All's well, Chang. I discovered quite a lot . . . Come quickly, we mustn't stay here . . . I'll put you in the picture . . .

Midnight tomorrow? . . . I'll come with you . . .

No, Chang, I think it's better if I go alone . . . I'll tell you why . . .

The next night . . .

(185)

Careful, there they are!

Is that the last lot?

Yes, just these to be loaded, and we can go . . .

So far so good . . .

Take the opium out of the barrel, get inside . . . and Bob's your uncle . . .

OK, we can move off now . . .

Meanwhile . . .

It was a mistake to pit your wits against mine, my dear Wang! . . . A big mistake! . . . But it's too late now . . . The time has come for you to die!

You smile? . . . You think it's like a thriller, don't you? . . . The hero rushes in at the last moment and saves your life . . . Pardon my laughter! . . . At this very moment your hero Tintin is already in my power!

We've been going for two hours . . . I wonder where to . . .

So you can abandon all hope! . . . They say the Chinese aren't afraid to die. Well, I've prepared a fitting end for you! . . . Your son, Wang, your own mad son, will cut off your head! . . . Picture the scene . . . Your wife, Tintin, and you, all beheaded by your son! . . .

Ah, it's you, Yamato! . . . All went well?

Like clockwork, Master . . . The barrels are in there . . .

Please enter, dear Mr Wang! . . . We don't want you to miss the show!

Now for some fun!

That's the one, Master . . . marked with a cross . . .

My dear Tintin, welcome to the end of the road!

Something tells me you weren't expecting this sort of reception when you emerged!

Too true!

I knew perfectly well you were in the barrel . . . You were at the Blue Lotus last night . . . and had a good laugh at my expense, no doubt . . . You heard the orders I gave Yamato . . . Everything had gone your way . . . But one of my men saw you leave and alerted me.

I told myself you certainly wouldn't be able to resist such a good opportunity, so I set a trap. I told them to leave you alone, they loosened the top of one barrel, and everything happened as I'd foreseen!

Well done, Mr Mitsuhirato. You're quite a clever man!

Cleverer than you thought, anyway! . . . Ah, here's an old friend of yours . . . He doesn't want to miss your execution! . . .

?

We got him, Grand Master.

Mr Rastapopoulos!

Exactly!

Rastapopoulos! . . . Roberto Rastapopoulos! You've been trying to spike my guns for a long time . . . Me, Rastapopoulos, king of drug smugglers . . . Rastapopoulos, who went over a cliff near Gaipajama . . . and you thought I died . . . Rastapopoulos, alive and well . . . And as always, coming out on top . . .

You, leader of the gang? . . . Impossible!

Bring in the others, Yamato . . .

You aren't convinced, eh? . . . Look at that! . . . Now do you believe me? . . .

The sign of the Pharaoh Kih-Oskh!*

Here, take this. It's for you . . .

Lao Tzu said: You must find the way' . . . I've found it . . . It's quite easy. I'm going to cut off your head. Then you too will know the truth . . .

You're . . . you're absolutely sure there isn't any risk for us? . . .

No, as soon as he's done the job Yamato will take care of him . . .

* See Cigars of the Pharaoh

(187)

BANG

??? ??? ???

Bravo, Chang! . . .

Hands up! . . .

Victory!

Only just in time, Chang! I thought you hadn't succeeded . . .

Yes, it went without a hitch. The crew of the 'Harika Maru' didn't have time to say 'Ouch'! . . .

I bow my old head in respect before the courage of your youth, Chang!

Now you are free, Mrs Wang!

Well, gentlemen! It's my turn to do the explaining, Mr Mitsuhirato . . . Were you really silly enough to believe I'd walk straight into the lion's jaws? . . . You must think I'm a very simple soul! . . .

I knew perfectly well I'd been seen leaving the Blue Lotus. Nonetheless, I decided to visit godown No. 9 but I took a few precautions . . . Last night, the crew of the 'Harika Maru' were surprised by the Sons of the Dragon and put in irons. Some of our friends hid in the barrels to be delivered to you. Others waited for your men, then gave them a hand unloading the barrels . . . You know the rest . . .

Three men stay here to keep guard over the prisoners. The others search the house. Chang and I will go this way . . .

Great snakes! We've come out through a safe! . . .

What a funny smell! . . . It's like . . . Opium, isn't it? . . .

The Blue Lotus! . . .

SHANGHAI NEWS
上海報

FANG HSI-YING FOUND: Professor Prisoner in Opium Den

SHANGHAI, Wednesday:
Professor Fang Hsi-ying has been found! The good news was flashed to us this morning.

Last week eminent scholar Fang disappeared on his way home from a party given by a friend. Police efforts to trace him were unavailing. No clues were found.

Professor Fang Hsi-ying pictured just after his release.

Young European reporter Tintin joined in the hunt for the missing man of science. Earlier we reported incidents involving Tintin and the occupying Japanese forces. Secret society Sons of the Dragon aided Tintin in the rescue. Fang Hsi-ying was kidnapped by an international gang of drug smugglers, now all safely in police custody.

A wireless transmitter was found by police at Blue Lotus opium den. The transmitter was used by the drug smugglers to communicate wth their ships on the high seas. Information radioed included sea routes, ports to be avoided, points of embarkation and uploading.

Home of Japanese subject Mitsuhirato was also searched. No comment, say police on reports of seizure of top-secret documents. Unconfirmed rumours suggest the papers concern undercover political activity by a neighbouring power. Speculation mounts that they disclose the recent Shanghai-Nanking railway incident as a pretext for extended Japanese occupation. League of Nations officials in Geneva will study the captured documents.

TINTIN'S OWN STORY

This morning, hero of the hour Mr Tintin, talked to us about his adventures.

Tintin, rescuer of Professor Fang Hsi-ying, with Snowy, his faithful companion.

The young reporter is the guest of Mr Wang Chen-yee at his host's picturesque villa on the Nanking road.

When we called, our hero, young and smiling, greeted us wearing Chinese dress. Could this really be the scourge of the terrible Shanghai gangsters?

After our greetings and congratulations, we asked Mr Tintin to tell us how he succeeded in smashing the most dangerous organisation.

Mr Wang, a tall, elderly, venerable man with an impish smile said:
"You must tell the world it is entirely due to him that my wife, my son and I are alive today!"

With these words our interview was concluded, and we said farewell to the friendly reporter and his kindly host.

L.G.T.

Young people carry posters of Tintin through Shanghai streets.

The conclusions of the Sub-Committee leave no room for doubt. The documents seized in Shanghai provide irrefutable proof. The attack upon the Shanghai-Nanking railway was planned and executed by a Japanese subject working upon direct orders from his government! . . .

I shall be interested to hear the Japanese delegate's reply . . .

Me, too . . . Look, he's going to speak now . . .

Gentlemen, make no mistake! I categorically deny the accusations contained in the report of the 873rd Sub-Committee. These accusations are an insult to which Japan declines to make any response other than silence and contempt! Nevertheless, to prove that the integrity of my country is beyond doubt . . .

. . . I am authorised to announce that my government has ordered its troops to withdraw from Chinese territories occupied after the incident on the Shanghai-Nanking railway. To that, gentlemen, I must add with regret that in solemn protest against the affront to my country, Japan finds herself obliged to resign from the League of Nations!

WAY OUT

Meanwhile, in Shanghai . . .

I have wonderful news for you: my son is cured! . . . Professor Fang Hsi-ying has discovered an antidote to the terrible poison of madness! . . .

He has? . . . Oh, how glad I am!

Venerable Master, two gentlemen wish to speak to Mr Tintin.

Good morning . . . Er . . . Here we are at last . . .

To be precise: good morning. Here we are, last as usual . . .

Um . . . er . . . So here you are? . . .

Yes, we've come . . . to offer our congratulations, and to tell you we . . . we . . .

We never believed for a minute you were guilty. But what could we do? We had to obey orders . . .

It makes me sick! Having to help celebrate the triumph of that little snake!

What else do you think we can do?

Look, Tintin! . . . Read this . . .

THE BLUE LOTUS AFFAIR

MITSUHIRATO COMMITS HARA-KIRI

Shanghai, Saturday: Mr Mitsuhirato, implicated in the Blue Lotus affair and principal organiser of the attack on the Shangha Nankin railwa

Poor devil! . . . Still, he was a real villain!

That reminds me . . . I'm glad to see you completely recovered from your fall.

Our fall? . . . What fall? . . .

Oh, yes, our famous fall in 'Hukow!

Oh, yes, our fall in Hukow! . . . Yes, yes, now I remember! . . .

Yes, we're fully recovered now. How could we come such a cropper? We've never fallen so low! . . .

We shan't forget that downfall . . . We've learnt our lesson. We'll be careful in future!

You can be sure we shan't fall for that again!

No, we'll be keeping our eyes open, never fear!

Now it's time to go. We must leave you.

Already?

Au revoir! . . .

Goodbye! . . .

. . . I raise my glass to your precious health, Tintin. Your courage and nobility have restored happiness to this humble house. Your memory will be engraved upon our hearts as in finest crystal . . .

There is one who, if such is possible, will miss you even more than I. Chang, who has already known the sadness of losing his parents. Chang, who found in you a brother. If he wishes, he will be my son, the brother of my own poor son to whom our honourable friend Fang Hsi-ying has restored his reason . . .

What is the matter, Chang?

There is a rainbow in my heart, Venerable Lady . . . I weep because Tintin is going but the sun shines because I have a new mother and father!

Farewell, noble Tintin. May other friendships lighten your days in your country in the West, and accompany you along the way!

The next morning . . .

Goodbye, Tintin . . . Good luck go with you!

I wish the same for you, Chang! . . . Goodbye!

TOOOOT

TOOOOT